THORA
to: Abby J. M. Han

P9-DHF-236

703-528-2771

THORA belongs to
Abby Han.

Phone no.: 703-528-2771

Thank You!
Please Return.

THORA

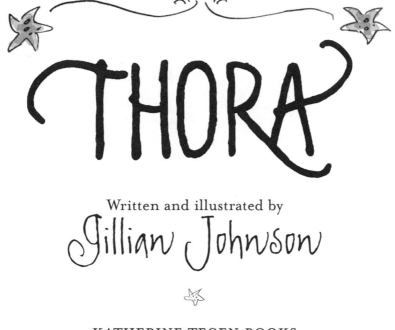

THORA

Written and illustrated by

Jillian Johnson

KATHERINE TEGEN BOOKS
An Imprint of HarperCollins*Publishers*

Thora

Copyright © 2003 by Gillian Johnson
 Printed in the United States of America. For information address HarperCollins Children's Books, a division of HarperCollins Publishers, 1350 Avenue of the Americas, New York, NY 10019.
www.harperchildrens.com

Library of Congress Cataloging-in-Publication Data
Johnson, Gillian.
　Thora / written and illustrated by Gillian Johnson.— 1st U.S. ed.
　p. cm.
　Summary: Ten-year-old Thora, daughter of a mermaid mother and a human father, has many adventures at sea until she must return to the seaside town of Grimli and save her mother, who has been captured by the greedy real estate developer Frooty de Mare.
　ISBN 0-06-074378-6 — ISBN 0-06-074379-4 (lib. bdg.)
　[1. Mermaids—Fiction. 2. Friendship—Fiction. 3. Mothers and daughters—Fiction. 4. Magic—Fiction. 5. England—Fiction. 6. Humorous stories.] I. Title.
PZ7.G631775Th 2005
[Fic]—dc22
　　　　　　　　　　　　　　　　　　2004014904

Typography by Karin Paprocki
First U.S. edition, HarperCollins Publishers Inc., 2005
Originally published in Australia by HarperCollins*Publishers* Pty Limited, 2003
1 2 3 4 5 6 7 8 9 10
❖

For Ron Reichertz

THORA

Prologue

The trouble with humans
Is that their legs do not have scales
Their feet do not have flippers
Their heads don't blow like whales
Their swimming is atrocious
Their voices sound like rust
Their eyes are dimmed by air and often
Blinded by the dust.

The trouble with mermaids
Is that their tails do not have feet
Their fins do not have toes
And their legs are obsolete.
Their running is atrocious
Their voices sound like rain
Their eyes are dimmed by oceans
And they like to drink champagne.

This is what I told a mermaid
Who came to ask advice

(She'd fallen for
A man named Thor
And wondered at what price):

"Love between a mermaid
And a man without a tail
Will make you happy for a day
But then it has to fail.

"If you produce a child
— Half of the land and sea
It will have to live in both
In order to be free.

"Ten years at sea! Ten years on land!
Between two worlds this girl must stand!
And if this doesn't come to be"
(I told her rather peevishly)
"The gods will then meet secretly
They'll roll their eyes
They'll sip their tea
And who knows what
They will agree
for that
We'll have
To wait
And see."

The seaside town of Grimli

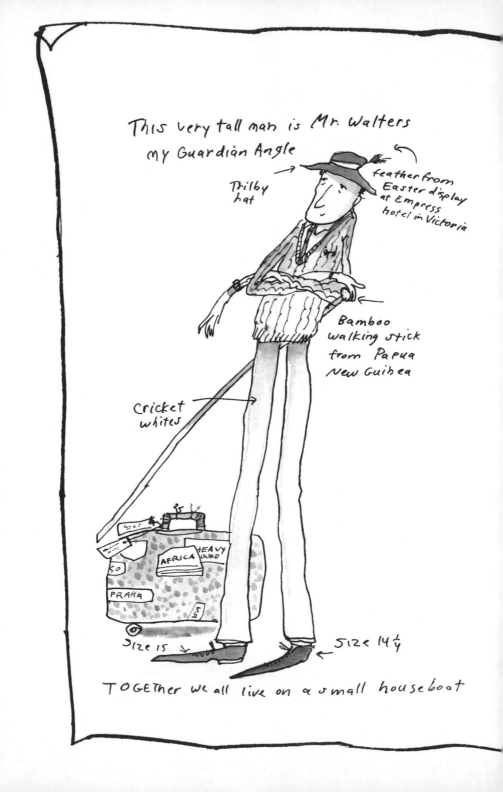

LOKI

OR at least we did
until we landed in a
small *seaside* town, GRIMLI,
to begin ten years of
life on land.

CHAPTER

1

IT ALL STARTED TEN YEARS AGO on a fine summer evening when a very tall man strolled along the Grimli pier. His name was Mr. Walters and he was not just tall, but very tall. He was so tall he could have been the president of the Tall Club. But he wasn't the president of anything anymore. He was retired, and he was headed for the end of the pier, where he planned to sit on the red oil drum and smoke his last cigar of the evening.

He never made it.

With only a few steps to go, he heard a rather unusual cry. He stopped and scanned the harbor. Eventually, his eyes came to rest on the old houseboat with the FOR SALE sign. The *Loki*.

He'd noticed it before, but had never paused to take a good look. What made him take notice now was not the rather odd construction of the boat, nor the peeling paint of its cabin or even the crooked way it sat in the water, but rather the loud noise coming out of it.

WAAAAAA! WAAAAAA! WAAAAAA!

He tiptoed over. The large main glass window was steamed up, and the curtains were drawn. Cupping his hand to his ear, he leaned his head against the front door and listened.

The crying was supernaturally loud.

It reminded him of all the worst things in life.

Dentist drills.

Cold showers.

Seasickness and creamed corn.

So why didn't he turn and run?

Mr. Walters had never much liked babies, but this was different. Though terrible, the sheer volume of the crying reminded him of the effort of Olympic champions in some of the great photo finishes of his day. There was something heroic—noble even—in its amplitude. It made him want to join.

He rapped on the cabin door. When nobody answered, he turned the metal door handle and gently let himself in.

Not once did it occur to him not to.

The room was dark and damp and smelled distinctly fishy. When his eyes adjusted to the darkness, he gasped. "Good gracious!"

Cut into the middle of the floor was a hole the size of an extra-large pepperoni pizza. The sea made a slurping sound as it splashed upward. There were puddles everywhere.

On the walls there were pictures of movie stars and posters advertising films. On the far side of the room stood a pile of dark furniture and a chest of drawers. The crying sound was coming from the opened bottom drawer. He rushed over.

WAAAAAA! WAAAAAA! WAAAAAA!

Tucked into a wad of wet, green seaweed was a shrieking baby.

His first thought was that the creature must be very cold, because its legs were quite purple.

He scooped it up. Immediately the noise stopped and the baby opened one green eye. There was a click and a whooosh, and then a thin but powerful jet of water sprayed up and knocked his hat clear off his head. "Ratbag!" he cried, stuffing the creature back into the drawer, where it resumed its crying, harder and louder than before.

It was at that moment that Mr. Walters noticed a hole on the top of the baby's bald head. It was no bigger than one of the foreign coins he tossed into wishing wells the world over.

And that was not all. The legs were scaly and the hands were most definitely webbed.

"Deary me," he whispered.

The baby kicked and thrashed.

WAAAAAAAA! WAAAAAA! WAAAAAA!

How could he get it to stop? Should he sing it a song? He couldn't hold a tune.

Change the diaper? He didn't know how.

Hang the baby from the ceiling by its toes? What if it started to leak from the hole in its head?

Suddenly the baby reached up and grabbed his hand.

Mr. Walters jumped back. Then he laughed. "I know what you need," he said. "Won't be a minute . . . you stay right where you are."

WAAAAAAAAA!

CHAPTER
2

MANY HUNDREDS OF LEAGUES BENEATH THE *Loki*, Halla made her way along the ocean floor to the home where she had grown up.

Two kilograms of fresh squid cheeks and an abalone shell filled with sea cucumber juice—Thora had refused it all.

Halla had been trying for days to feed her baby. Shark meat. Tuna. Crab's legs. A pudding of caviar and seal blubber. Nothing worked. Nothing stopped Thora's incessant cries. Neither child nor mother had slept for days.

CHAPTER
3

IT WAS GETTING LATE AND THE shops in Grimli were
closed, but a butter-colored light shone in the windows of
the Allbent Cinema. Three women, sisters, were huddled
around a blackboard. One of them was writing something.
At the sound of the knock, they looked up, startled.

A very tall man peered in at them. He removed his hat
and gave a sort of bow. "Good evening," he said through
the glass.

The effect was courtly. One of the sisters, Flossie,
judged the man a perfect gent. He had gentle, triangular
eyes and a voice right out of the movies. She trembled when
she heard his English accent. Hadn't she seen him in a
recent film? She checked her pocket for a pen. She might
ask him for his autograph.

"What do you want?" asked Lottie briskly. She was tall
and wishbone thin.

Dottie giggled nervously.

"I'm terribly sorry to disturb you," he said, squinting up at the large clock on the wall, "especially at this late hour . . . but I wondered if you might . . . I wonder if you have any milk for a baby?" He regarded them with surprised eyes, as if he didn't quite believe what he was saying.

"Yes," he added hastily. "The baby is very hungry, and all the shops are closed."

"Baby?"

"Yes." He nodded politely.

The sisters looked relieved. They unlocked the doors and welcomed him in.

"Girl or boy?" asked Flossie.

Mr. Walters had no idea. The image of the baby's face

floated up before his eyes. "Girl," he guessed.

The sisters consulted one another. Then Dottie and Lottie excused themselves and went off to fetch some supplies.

Flossie smoothed her skirt. "Is the baby your granddaughter?"

"In a manner of speaking," he replied.

Flossie stared at him hard. "Are you an actor by any chance?" she asked.

"Good heavens, no," he replied.

"I feel I've seen you somewhere," she said. "Or *heard* you . . ."

"Really?" said Mr. Walters. He looked over at the blackboard. Under the word *Banished* was a name: Frooty de Mare.

"An unfortunate name," he said, changing the subject.

"It suits him," said Flossie.

At that moment, Dottie and Lottie returned carrying a large basket. It contained a bottle of milk, a thermos filled with extra milk (warmed to just the right temperature), a soft gray and yellow blanket, an ancient-looking blue bunny rabbit with a bell around its neck, and finally, a silver rattle in the shape of a dumbbell.

Mr. Walters could not be sure, but he thought he saw tears in Dottie's eyes as she explained how to use the glass bottle. "Everything is plastic now," she said. "But these old bottles are much nicer to drink from. My son used them over twenty years ago."

"Dottie can't throw anything away," said Flossie.

"Are you sure it's all right?" asked Mr. Walters.

"Yes," sniffed Dottie. "The time has come."

The two others nodded. They wished him and the little one well. Then Flossie walked him to the door.

"Hope we see you again," she said with a wink.

Blushing, Mr. Walters hurried back to the *Loki*.

CHAPTER

4

THE BACK WINDOW WAS OPEN. HALLA found her mother and grandmother in the living room.

"Can't help you," said her mother coldly. She pressed a button on the wall. An alarm sounded.

Her grandmother buried her face in her hands and rocked in her rocking chair.

Her father swam into the room. "What's going on in here?" When he saw his daughter, he narrowed his eyes. *"I have no daughter! Take her away!"*

A reluctant squid guard showed her the way out and slammed the gate in her face.

All her old friends had swum the other way when they saw her.

All but her best friend.

Marina required no explanation. She took Halla's hand. "The Sea Shrew might help you."

CHAPTER

5

THE BABY WAS STILL HOWLING. MR. WALTERS stooped over her basket. With a nervous hand, he tilted the bottle up and placed the rubber part in her mouth. A little bit of milk dribbled out, but her eyes clamped shut and she latched on. Silence.

"Good girl," he whispered. "You *are* a girl?"

While she drank, Mr. Walters folded the blanket and draped it over the edge of the drawer. He tucked the bunny rabbit next to her. He set the extra milk on the kitchen counter. Then he lit a cigar and pushed a chair up beside the baby to sit and watch.

When she had drained the bottle, she opened her eyes and belched.

In that instant, Mr. Walters felt his heart spring open. And before he could shut it again, the little baby with the supernatural cry, the violet legs, and the hole in her head the size of an Icelandic krona climbed into it and fell asleep. On her face, a look of utter contentment.

The rummy cigar smoke swirled through the room.

He had not realized until that moment how lonely his life had been. For the first time since before his wife had died, he felt truly happy.

CHAPTER 6

THE SEA SHREW ROLLED HER EYES when she saw Halla.

"I knew I would see you again, you numbskull. Marrying a human! Well, he's gone now, isn't he? And you are left with a half-human child. Did you expect it to work out differently?"

Halla looked down at her tail. "I don't know what to do. The baby's been crying for five days."

"I know. I can hear her. It's obnoxious!"

"How do I get her to stop?"

"Feed her!"

"She won't take my milk. I think it might be too salty."

"Give her human food, you idiot!"

Halla ignored the old woman's taunts. "How do I raise a half-human child? Please? I have no idea what to do!"

"You want practical advice? Go to your mother." The

Shrew ran her fingers through her wiry gray hair. "I talk destiny."

"What *is* her destiny?" asked Marina quickly.

The Sea Shrew sat very still and closed her eyes. Then in a superior voice she began to speak. "If she can live between worlds for ten years, this daughter of hers can live. Otherwise, mother and daughter will go the way of the human husband."

Marina squeezed Halla's hand. "What happened to him?"

Halla frowned. "Don't know."

"Is he alive?"

"If the gods are kind," whispered Halla.

"Listen up," said the old hag. "Unions between humans and mermaids are forbidden, Halla, you knew that. Now you must pay. Very few can live between worlds. On your daughter's tenth birthday, you must deliver her back to the land. To the world of her father." The Shrew smiled enigmatically and added: *"If she lives that long."*

If mermaids could cry, Halla would have flooded the seas.

"How fascinating," said the Shrew suddenly, gazing upward.

"What?" asked Halla.

"Your daughter has stopped crying."

The Sea Shrew's words did not reassure Halla.

"Don't be upset," said Marina as they swam off. "She's a nasty old drama queen."

Halla gave her friend a hug and headed back to the World Above.

To the *Loki*.

And to her newborn baby, Thora.

CHAPTER
7

THE FIRST THING HALLA NOTICED AS she swam up toward the *Loki* was the silence.

It was like the quiet at the bottom of the Merino Trench, so silent it was deafening.

She swam as fast as she could, a creeping chill in the pit of her stomach. No matter how much seawater she gulped, her throat felt dry.

How could she manage to feed her child human food? Where would it come from? How? It was all *impossible*!

It seemed to take forever, but finally she surfaced in the harbor and slipped silently under the *Loki* and up through the pizza-sized hole.

The cigar smoke confused her. She wondered for an instant if she had surfaced in the wrong boat.

But no.

She raised herself up on her arms and peered over at her child.

Thora's cheeks were pink. Her eyes closed. There was a smile on her lips.

The regular little breaths were the sweetest music Halla had ever heard.

"My dear woman," came a human voice through the smoke.

A vision in white. Like a ghost. A very tall, very thin ghost.

"Can I give you a hand?"

He had a kindly, creased face with a long, hooked nose.

"Mr. Jack Walters," he whispered, extending his hand.

"I heard your baby crying. . . . I assume it is yours? Yes? Good. Girl? Yes. Good. I couldn't help but worry. Oh, dear. Now *you* look worried. Don't be scared. I am very sorry for trespassing. I don't know what came over me! I'll leave immediately. I was just concerned that this little baby . . . your child, that is . . . seemed hungry, hungry enough to eat my hand."

His eyes fell on Halla's tail. "Good gracious me!"

Not for the first time that evening, Mr. Walters gaped. His eyes nearly popped out of their sockets.

"Buying the boat, are you?" she asked sadly.

"Nooooo." Mr. Walters shook his head, his eyes still fastened on her tail.

She believed him. "Never seen a mermaid?"

"No."

"Well, you have now." Halla motioned to the baby. "How did you get her to go to sleep?"

"Milk."

"What sort?"

Mr. Walters looked worried. "I'm not entirely sure," he said. "Is there more than one sort? I'm not very experienced at this sort of thing. I suppose it's cow's milk." He held up the milk bottle. "There's more right here."

Human food. "Thank you." Halla rested on her arms,

tail in the water. "Sorry to be rude." She closed her eyes. "But I'm so very tired."

As she drifted off to sleep, she sensed Mr. Walters slip a pillow under her head. She heard the words "pumpkin pie." The creak of floorboards. The click of the door.

WHAT ON EARTH WOULD HAPPEN TO the mermaid and her baby?

This is what Mr. Walters pondered the next morning as he ironed his cricket whites. He liked his trousers to keep their crease and so he traveled with a little portable electric iron.

In his rather long life, Mr. Walters had, as they say, done it all. Sailor, swimmer, coach, poet, journalist, cricket commentator. He'd fought in a war and he'd tried to write a book. Now that he was retired, he spent his time traveling around the world. And he liked to stay in small inns in out-of-the-way seaside towns where nobody recognized him. Where he could read and smoke his cigars without people hounding him for his autograph.

When he was dressed and packed, he called a taxicab and carried his bags down the steep stairs of the Blue Bell Bed and Breakfast.

His holiday was over.

"I've had a *marvelous* time," he said to Mrs. Valihora, the owner. "See you next year."

"You won't be staying *here,* Mr. Walters," she said. She set her mop against the wall and took his keys.

"What is it?" he asked. "Have I offended you?"

"No, no." Then Mrs. Valihora informed Mr. Walters that the Blue Bell was about to be knocked down. "The wrecking ball will be paying us a visit some time next month."

"How terrible!" said Mr. Walters.

"Yes. I would have told you sooner, but I didn't want to spoil your holiday."

Mr. Walters looked through the window at the crashing surf. Not far off, bobbing in the harbor, he could see the *Loki.* The image of the little baby floated up, as if on a screen, in his mind. Would she and her mother be safe?

"But there's nothing to be done," Mrs. Valihora continued.

"Why?"

"Ask Frooty de Mare," she said.

Mr. Walters recalled the blackboard at the cinema. "Who is he exactly?"

"Some call him an entrepreneur. I call him a shark. He's buying up all the seafront property. He wants to put us all out of business."

"What is he going to build?"

"The rumor is that he wants to flatten the cinema and replace it with one of his horrible hotels. He's already got the name: The Tooty Frooty."

"Dreadful," said Mr. Walters.

"But there's a fly in the ointment."

"What's that?"

"The Greenberg sisters won't sell."

"Ah, the Greenberg sisters." Mr. Walters nodded. "And why not?"

Mrs. Valihora: "I figure they love the movies too much."

The old journalist in him quickened. "So how do you explain Frooty's ambition?"

"Frooty's father left when he was very young," she began. "Frooty and his mother suffered. They both had to go out to work—Mrs. de Mare cleaned houses and Frooty took whatever he could—hard jobs sweeping up fish guts, that sort of thing. They were not the first people to have a difficult life, but somehow with Frooty, you never felt very

23

sorry for him. He was always full of himself and very pushy. But he worked devilishly hard, and nobody was surprised when he was made a manager at the fish plant." She paused. "But there was something warped about his drive. He proved himself, but it wasn't enough. Next thing you know, he *owns* the factory. Then the land surrounding it. Now he wants to buy up the whole town!"

"But how could he afford to do that?"

"Fishing. He owns the fleets. This is a poor town. People want cash, and he's always got lots."

There was a honk.

"There's your taxi," said Mrs. Valihora.

Mr. Walters tipped his hat and, as he carried out his bags, his gaze once again fell on the *Loki*. He imagined one of Frooty de Mare's wrecking balls smashing it to bits. A flicker of anger cleared his mind.

He had an idea.

CHAPTER
9

"AIRPORT?" SAID THE CAB DRIVER.

"Not yet," said Mr. Walters. "I want to stop first at the pier. The *Loki*. Do you know it?"

"Sure," said the driver. "It's an old houseboat that used to belong to a local lad. He disappeared without a trace last Christmas."

"How terrible!" exclaimed Mr. Walters. "What happened to him?"

The driver glanced at him suspiciously. "You ask a lot of questions, mister."

"Just curious."

"There're lots of different theories about what *might* have happened."

"Do tell."

The cab driver pressed a button. Water squirted out onto the windshield. Then he switched on the wipers. "Okay then. One theory was that he eloped and ran off to

25

Bora-Bora. Another was that he pulled the old *vamoose* act. You know, skadaddled. *Bye-bye folks, I'm gonzo.*"

Mr. Walters looked confused.

The driver shook his head. "Then there's the sorts of stories that you hear but don't believe."

"Such as?"

"I'm not saying *I* believe them."

"Yes . . . ?"

"I mean I'm a reasonable person. . . ."

"*Come on*, dear chap."

The driver shrugged. "I heard that he'd fallen for a mermaid."

Mr. Walters sat bolt upright, hitting his head on the cab ceiling and squashing his hat. "Yes?"

"A lot of rubbish. But these stories spring up when a person disappears. Anyway, everybody says now that Frooty de Mare is going to buy the *Loki*—if he hasn't already."

"Why does Frooty de Mare want the boat?"

The driver groaned. "He doesn't want the *boat*—it's worth diddly-squat. He wants the lease on the *berth*. If he owns that lease, then he owns the entire harbor, because he's already bought all the other leases. Next to the cinema, this is the most valuable real estate in town. *I'd* buy it if I could. Anyway, no drama really. He's probably the only one in town who can pay cash for it. Money talks. I'm telling you, I picked the wrong profession."

In the backseat of the cab, Mr. Walters felt the way he had when the Greek cheat Stavros Constaninopolis won an Olympic medal he didn't deserve.

"If I wanted to buy the *Loki* and its lease, where would I go?"

"Seriously?"

"Yes."

The car did a U-turn. Tires squealing, the taxi headed through an empty parking lot and pulled up opposite a small, redbrick house with white trim. A sign in the window read HARBORMASTER.

CHAPTER
10

HALLA NEARLY JUMPED OUT OF HER scales.

Rap! Rap! Rap!

The FOR SALE sign had been posted by the harbormaster a few months before Thora's birth. After Thor disappeared, his mother had paid the dues for six months in the hope that Thor would return. When he did not, the *Loki* was put up for sale. Thor's mother had wanted to buy it but was reminded by caring relatives of the following facts:

· She did not have the money.

· She knew nothing about boats.

To make it all a little bit easier, she had made one special request: The boat must not be sold to Frooty de Mare. *No matter what.* So far the harbormaster had managed to honor her request. But Frooty was applying some serious pressure.

From the water, Halla had watched the houseboat hunters come and go. Jolly folk in sunglasses and deck shoes. Once she'd returned from an outing to find the furniture pushed against the wall. The fridge cleaned out. The windows polished. She had no way of knowing when they were coming, or how long they'd stay. Usually they didn't even knock.

She slipped the baby into her bed and pushed the bottom drawer three-quarters shut. Immediately Thora began to cry.

"Drat," whispered Halla.

Rap! Rap! Rap!

She scooped Thora out of her seaweed bed and held her tight. "Shhh," she whispered in her ear. She was about to slip into the water when she smelled the spicy cigar smoke from the night before. Her heart lifted. "Mr. Walters?" she asked cautiously.

The door opened. In the crack of light, she saw the vision in white. The kindly creased face. Long nose. He reminded Halla of the enormous, majestic sea horses that guarded the castle where she had grown up at the bottom of the sea, back when she was welcome in her parents' home.

Thora had stopped crying, and regarded Mr. Walters with wide eyes and a broad, toothless smile.

"Sorry to bother you again, my dear woman, but I've been giving your situation some thought." He rattled a set of keys. "I just bought the *Loki*. I wondered if we might have a chat?"

CHAPTER

11

ONCE AGAIN MR. WALTERS ASKED HALLA to repeat, word for word, what the Sea Shrew had said.

They spoke in whispers so as not to wake the sleeping baby.

This time he wrote it down in a small notebook that he used to record cricket scores.

> If she can live between worlds for ten years, this daughter of hers can live. Otherwise, mother and daughter will go the way of the human husband...

He lit a cigar and let the words swirl around him.

Halla rested on her elbows, her tail in the water. The words "live between worlds" had become a riddle. A riddle that was much more difficult than the cryptic crossword in the *Daily Seasider* that her husband, Thor, had said he loved to solve.

"Now explain to me how you got here," said Mr. Walters gently. "I need to know the whole story."

"Ever since I was very small," began Halla, "I wanted to visit the World Above."

Mr. Walters nodded.

"I'd heard so many mysterious stories about blue skies and clouds and wind and air. About people with two legs and bicycles and strange things to eat like popcorn and cotton candy. I guess I just wanted to experience all these things for myself."

"Understandable," said Mr. Walters.

"Also, I have always been a little claustrophobic. As if the water pressed down more heavily on me than it did my friends. I dreamed about the lightness of dry hair, of *air*." She took a deep breath. "Of course, my parents were against the whole idea of the World Above. You know . . . 'look what happened to the Little Mermaid' sort of thing. Well, one day, after I'd argued with them about it, I decided to surface on my own. On my way up, I ran into trouble. My tail got tangled up in some human garbage, an old plastic bag. Using just my arms, I somehow surfaced. The first thing I saw was the Rock."

She pointed to the large black rock about five miles out in the water. Mr. Walters, who was a little shortsighted, squinted out to sea and nodded.

"As I made my way there, I heard a shout. Then I felt a sharp pain in my tail, right about here." She pointed to a silvery patch where the scales were a lighter color. "I'd been hooked by a fisherman. He freed me, first from the hook and then the garbage bag. He helped me to the Rock and, when I'd caught my breath, he told me to return home. To go back where I came from. I asked him if I might touch his hair. It was dry! And he had two legs and no scales whatsoever! The man was Thor. He was out for an evening of fishing after a shift at the cinema, where he worked as the projectionist. I knew the dangers and so did he. Then he said that my hair smelled of pumpkin pie—I didn't know what that was, but it sounded delicious. In that moment, he seemed to me the most poetic creature I'd ever met and the World Above the most magical. The clouds that evening were fat and fluffy, and the air was warm and dry. I wanted to stay. To be with him forever. But five days after we married, well . . . it was raining very hard. . . . He was meeting someone, I think. . . . He never returned."

"You've heard nothing since?"

"Not a word."

"Terrible," said Mr. Walters.

"Yes." Halla blinked. "I lived in and around the boat for the next nine months, waiting for him to come back. I was too frightened to think straight. I just let myself float along, hoping he would return. When it occurred to me that he was not going to, I lost my shimmer. I couldn't come up with a plan. Time passes quickly when you're not in a rush."

Mr. Walters nodded.

"Thora was born a week ago." Halla let her hair fall into her eyes so he could not see her distress. "I love her more than anything, and yet I don't know how to raise her."

Truth was, Mr. Walters was a little worried too. For one thing, he was no authority on raising children—or half-mermaids for that matter. Also, he had spent most of his retirement savings on the boat and its lease. Furthermore, he was supposed to be back in England right now, attending the Wimbledon finals. He would be missing some *cracking* good tennis.

On the other hand, something had led him here, to this town, to this boat, to this mermaid and her half-mermaid daughter. They were depending on him. They needed him.

It was too late to turn back.

"Halla," he said, a little awkwardly. "Everything is going to be all right." As he said it, he believed it. For the first time, Mr. Walters was not the journalist, or the cricket commentator, or the swimming official. He was what he was. A retired old geezer with time on his hands and the desire to help a mermaid in distress. They had a place to live. Now they needed a way to support themselves. A way to live half on land, half on sea. None of his worries did he mention to Halla. Not yet, anyway. "The World Above will be a lot less murky after a good night's sleep."

Halla frowned slightly, but she nodded. "Sleep is a good idea."

CHAPTER

12

FROOTY DE MARE WAS GOBSMACKED WHEN he learned that
the *Loki* and its ninety-nine-year lease had been sold right
under his great big nose!

He paced up and down the corridor in the harbormaster's office grilling the harbormaster's assistant. This was
the first time in years that anybody outside Grimli had
bought a property. People from elsewhere simply didn't
do that. He couldn't believe it. "What was the shyster's
name?"

"He called himself Walters."

"I don't understand you people. First you tell me there
will be delays. Then you tell me there will be more delays.
Then you go and sell the blasted thing. *To someone else.* It's
not fair!"

"I'm only following orders, sir."

"That boss of yours has some explaining to do. I can't
build up this two-bit harbor unless I own *each* and *every*

berth. I have a lot of money riding on this project. Big money. Bigger money than you'll ever know about. *I'm in the big leagues, buster.*"

Terror flashed in the assistant's eyes. "He paid in cash."

"I don't care if he paid in pink Cadillacs. I need that lease!"

CHAPTER
13

THE NEXT MORNING, MR. WALTERS SAT on a deck chair watching Halla swim circles in the harbor with her infant daughter in her arms. She was swimming so fast that Mr. Walters grew dizzy. Suddenly it came to him—an idea so perfect, so practical, and so *possible*, that he began to laugh. He retrieved his stopwatch from his bag and waved at Halla to come over.

"How long might it take you to swim to shore and back again?"

Halla shrugged. "Not sure."

She handed Thora over to Mr. Walters and set off. In no time at all, she was back again.

"Extraordinary," said Mr. Walters. She was not even out of breath!

"What about to the Rock?"

For Halla it was an amusing game. She grinned and pushed off. He watched her glide through the water, the power of her tail propelling her soundlessly as a seal, her arms reaching gracefully as if she were saluting starfish on a summer's day.

Yes, Halla reminded Mr. Walters of the great open-water swimmer Marcella von Ditz. The only female to cross the Great Gonzo River in Mexico, the Bermuda Triangle, and Bass Strait. He had reported all three achievements on the BBC.

It took Halla less than twenty minutes to swim to the Rock and back again. "A world record," whispered Mr. Walters into Thora's ear. "Without a doubt."

"I say, my dear, have you ever considered competitive swimming?"

"What's that?" asked Halla.

Mr. Walters triangular eyes lit up. This was one of his favorite topics.

He told Halla that swimming had a long and honorable human history.

"People *love* water. They bathe, shower, swim, dive, boat, float, race. They compete in swimming pools for medals and ribbons and silver trays and pen sets and professional sponsorships. They also swim across lakes, down rivers, and in seas. They've always done it. They probably always will."

Halla was amazed. "You're telling me that humans actually swim across lakes and rivers for *money*?"

Mr. Walters tried to consider the idea from a mermaid's point of view. "Perhaps it seems a little . . . well, silly, to you . . . but yes, it is not uncommon for a talented swimmer to live very comfortably off their winnings."

Halla looked a little overcome. "It's tragic, really," she said.

"What do you mean?" said Mr. Walters.

"Human beings are so badly designed for water." She held up her hand. "No webbing. No gills. And legs must be a dreadful burden. My husband, Thor, told me that humans have to hold their breath or else they'll drown."

"Well, yes."

"Once I saw some people swimming down by the sea floor with 'Club Med' written on their suits. Thor said they were scuba divers. They were so loaded down with equipment—face masks and tanks on their backs and long plastic flippers on their feet—that I can't see how they were enjoying themselves. They swam off when they saw me."

She looked down at her tail and sighed. "Then again, I suppose I'm not very well designed for land."

"No," agreed Mr. Walters. "But your child is. And our challenge is for you and Thora to live not on land, but *between worlds*. To be of both land and water. Swimming races might be just our ticket."

"It seems too easy."

"Easy?" said Mr. Walters. "Nothing worth doing is easy. You will have to hide your tail. Adapt to different water temperatures. Find ways to persuade people you are human. Also, it won't always be easy for Thora. It will mean constant travel. She will have to live on the *Loki*. Speak different languages. Adapt. But I will be able to help. I know a fair amount about the way these competitions are run. If you win prize money, we'll take just what we need and donate the rest to the charity of your choice. I'll be the middleman. And as Thora's guardian grandfather, I can take care of the human side of things."

"They really give *prize money* for swimming across a river? It just sounds so far-fetched."

"Does that mean you'll give it a try?"

"I'd be crazy not to."

41

That evening, Mr. Walters made some telephone calls to his friends around the world. In the morning, he handed Halla a list of open-water competitions. "The prize money is very good these days!"

There was no time to waste. The open-water swimming season was already under way. The first race was to be held on the Thames in England.

The odd little family set sail in the *Loki* immediately.

CHAPTER
14

FROOTY DE MARE TOOK A DEEP BREATH of clean, crisp Grimli air.

He would bottle it and call it "Champagne by the Sea." Sell it for twenty dollars a pop. Frooty prided himself on his good ideas. He considered himself a genius.

Meanwhile, he needed to sort out this *Loki* business. He would act like a professional. He would stay calm. The best businessmen didn't lose their temper, although sometimes geniuses did.

These were his thoughts as he headed by foot to the *Loki* to have a little chat with this Walters character.

He paused to survey the coastline. He felt like an artist facing a vast blank canvas, poised to paint his masterpiece. In a few weeks' time, construction would begin on the Tooty Frooty. This boring stretch of coastline would be transformed into a snazzy seaside resort for discriminating holiday-goers with cash in their pockets. Once he got his

hands on the cinema's prime real estate, he'd start construction on the Fun House, a five-star hotel with a revolv-
ing restaurant and vibrating octopus-shaped beds. Then
there were the plans for the harbor. He had the name: *De
Mare's Magnificent Marina*. Yes, there was no shortage of good
ideas.

He just needed to solve this little glitch with the *Loki*.

But when he got there, the *Loki* was gone.

CHAPTER

15

MR. WALTERS CRADLED THE HOWLING THORA in the *Loki* as Halla swam and won the race down the Thames.

The English loved her. Even the competitors she'd beaten loved her. Her modesty appealed to everyone. She didn't wear makeup or act flash. She spoke in a quaint style with an accent that nobody was able to place. When asked where she was from, she merely shrugged and said, "The bottom of the sea. Why?" That response seemed to drive everybody wild. The television interview with the BBC went very well. Nobody found it odd that Halla insisted on speaking to the reporters from the pizza-shaped hole in the floor of the *Loki*.

"How are you going to celebrate tonight, Halla?"

"I think I'll make an octopus cheek casserole and perhaps a little later take my daughter, Thora, for a swim."

Her face appeared on the cover of a number of

45

magazines. It probably didn't hurt that she was, as one newspaper reporter pointed out, "rather photogenic." Her eyes were large and gray, and her hair was blonde and smelled faintly of pumpkin pie. Even those people who don't like the taste of pumpkin pie, or its damp and mushy texture, admit that it has a delicious smell.

After the success of her Thames swim, Halla was invited to swim some of the great lakes of the world. She swam Lake Baikal in Russia. Then Lake Lagoda by the Gulf of Finland and Lake Titicaca in Peru. She was invited to swim the Dead Sea, but the high salt content bothered her eyes, so she swam the Danube instead.

To escape the beady eyes of the officials, Halla wore a special mermaid-disguising wet suit. Mr. Walters had it flown in specially for her swim across Lake Geneva. Inspired by the swimming greats Esther Williams and Annette Kellerman, it gave the illusion of two legs. At the same time, it directed attention to Halla's very human-looking upper body. Dubbed "The Halla-Skin," it very quickly became a fashion item and was sold in beach and boating shops around the world. A child-size suit was made for Thora. Nobody would have guessed that underneath her Halla-Skin, Thora's legs were purple and covered in scales.

FROOTY DE MARE
P.O. BOX 100
GRIMLI-BY-THE-SEA
18 NOVEMBER

DEAR MR. WALTERS:

LET ME INTRODUCE MYSELF. MY NAME IS FROOTY DE MARE, CEO OF TOOTY FROOTY ENTERPRISES, GRIMLI. NO DOUBT YOU HAVE HEARD OF ME. I AM WHAT YOU MIGHT CALL "A BIG FISH IN A SMALL TOWN," A SUCCESSFUL AND PROSPEROUS FORCE IN THE COMMUNITY, A ROLE MODEL FOR THE YOUNG, AN INSPIRATION FOR THE OLD.

IT HAS COME TO MY ATTENTION THAT YOU ARE NOW THE PROUD OWNER OF THE <u>LOKI</u>. FIRST, LET ME CONGRATULATE YOU ON YOUR RECENT PURCHASE. I AM SURE YOU WILL ENJOY MANY HOURS OF SAILING PLEASURE.

NOW, MIGHT I ADDRESS A SMALL POINT? GIVEN THAT YOU HAVE CHOSEN AN EXCITING LIFE ABROAD, YOU WILL SURELY HAVE NO USE FOR THE <u>LOKI</u>'S NINETY-NINE-YEAR LEASE. IN FACT, I AM CERTAIN THAT IT IS A BURDEN FOR YOU TO OWN SOMETHING SO FAR AWAY AND SO UTTERLY USELESS TO YOU IN ANY PRACTICAL WAY.

I WOULD LIKE, THEREFORE, TO RELEASE YOU FROM THIS TIRESOME OBLIGATION AND OFFER TO TRANSFER THE LEASE INTO MY OWN NAME. I WILL ASSUME ALL RESPONSIBILITY FROM HENCE ON. YOU NEED ONLY SIGN THE ATTACHED FORM IN THE SPACE INDICATED. NO WITNESS REQUIRED.

I HUMBLY OFFER THIS SERVICE FREE OF CHARGE. (NO MESSY PAPER-WORK! NO PROCESSING FEE!)

AGAIN, MY VERY BEST TO YOU. PLEASE FIND FOR YOUR CONVENIENCE A SELF-ADDRESSED ENVELOPE ENCLOSED.

SINCERELY,
FROOTY DE MARE

21 November

Dear Mr. de Mare:

No thank you.

Sincerely,
Mr. J. Walters

CHAPTER
16

WITHIN A FEW YEARS, HALLA WAS known in the open-water swimming world as "Halla's Comet." She rarely appeared to be tired and was never cold. The jellyfish did not sting her. The sharks treated her respectfully. She had a superb swimming style and a unique splashless kick. She won dozens of gold medals and thousands of dollars. The *Loki* slowly filled with interesting and unique gifts and prizes—diamond-studded goggles from Zurich, gold-plated flippers, a tortoiseshell table, thirteen pen sets, and twenty-one silver trays.

The most beloved prize of all was a blue-necked Indian peacock named Cosmo from Flinders Island. Cosmo was Thora's constant companion, and the two of them always rode in the boat alongside Halla as she swam. Mr. Walters was in charge of sailing and steering the *Loki*.

Sometimes the races were very long and boring. Thora loved to dangle over the side of the boat and talk to her mother as she swam. Sometimes she read stories to her from one of the books that Mr. Walters kept in constant supply—*The Red Book of Dogs*, *Treasure Island*, *A Field Guide to Tasmanian Birds*, *The Mark Spitz Story*.

"Mom!" she shouted as Halla swam the Coral Sea near Vanuatu. "Did you know that a Tasmanian devil can chew through bone?"

In Savu Savu, Fiji, she developed an interest in polar bears—"Hollow fur!"—and in Martinique, she worried about the rabbits she'd seen aboard the Finnish yacht *Bad Weather*. "If they eat tomatoes, they can die!"

Thora's reading and chatter kept Halla awake as she swam the rivers and lakes of the world.

When Thora was five, she was caught drawing a duck-billed platypus on a clean, pressed pair of Mr. Walters's cricket whites.

"Here," said Mr. Walters. And he gave her the blank book in which he had always intended to write his great novel. "Draw your pictures in this."

"I don't want to write a novel," said Thora. "I want to write and draw my *life*."

"Excellent plan." Mr. Walters clapped. "I always prefer my books with pictures!"

Thora opened the book and stared at the blank page. Then, with one of Mr. Walters's special Josiah Mason fine point pens, she dipped her nib into the ink and wrote her name.

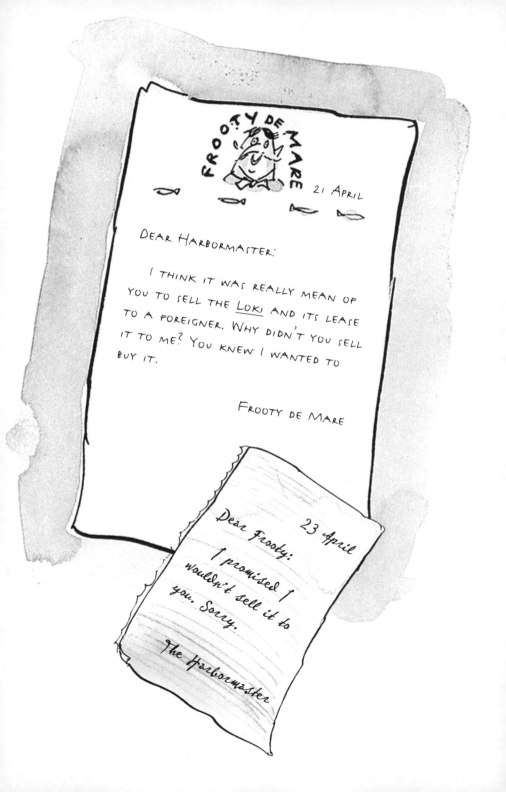

FROOTY DE MARE

25 APRIL

DEAR HM:

I SMELL A RAT. I CALL THIS DISCRIMINATION. I'M GOING TO REPORT YOU TO THE MAYOR.

FDM

26 April

Dear Frooty:

Take it on the chin. There are worse things.

The Harbormaster

FROOTY DE MARE

27 APRIL

DEAR MR. WALTERS:

PERHAPS YOU ARE A SHREWDER BUSINESSMAN
THAN MOST, BUT IT REMAINS MY SINCERE BELIEF THAT
YOU DO NOT MEAN TO REJECT MY LATEST OFFER TO
BUY THE NINETY-NINE-YEAR LEASE FOR THE <u>LOKI</u>.
I WOULD LIKE YOU TO NAME A PRICE SO WE CAN PUT
AN END TO THE FUN AND GAMES. IT IS TIME TO
MOVE FORWARD.

SINCERELY,
FROOTY DE MARE
CEO,
TOOTY FROOTY ENTERPRISES

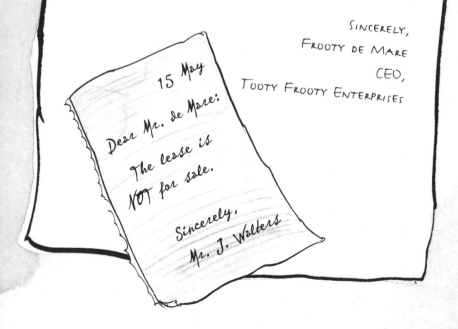

15 May

Dear Mr. de Mare:

The lease is
NOT for sale.

Sincerely,
Mr. J. Walters

FROOTY DE MARE

1 SEPTEMBER

DEAR MR. WALTERS:

THIS IS YOUR LAST CHANCE TO MAKE A HUGE PROFIT. SELL ME THE LEASE AND I WILL MAKE YOU A PARTNER IN MY COMPANY. ONLY A FOOLISH MAN WOULD DECLINE SUCH AN OFFER.

MR. FRUCTUS DE MARE
CEO,
TOOTY FROOTY ENTERPRISES

23 September
Dear Mr. de Mare:
Call me a foolish man. No thanks.

Mr. J. Walters

CHAPTER

17

"EVICT THEM?" ASKED THE MAYOR OF Grimli, Mr. Grimus Grubbs. "How?"

"Just tell the Greenbergs that the land belongs to the town council, issue them eviction notices, and kick them out. Do the same with Walters and his lease. Then sell them to me. I can make you a very rich man."

The mayor folded his arms across his chest and shook his head. "Impossible." For seven years, he had granted Frooty de Mare permits to build what he liked where he liked. For seven years, he'd let Frooty de Mare push him around. If the harbormaster could stand up to Frooty, so could he.

"You can't get your way," he said firmly. "For the *last* time, the lease to the *Loki* belongs to Walters. The cinema belongs to the Greenberg sisters. If they won't sell, there is nothing I can do. It would be against the law for me to evict them."

"So?"

"I can't do it."

"You mean you *won't* do it."

"That's correct."

The two men glared at each other.

Then Frooty looked out the vast office window at the orange neon glow from the Tooty Frooty Hotel and Seafood Restaurant, now seven years old. "Meany." He glowered.

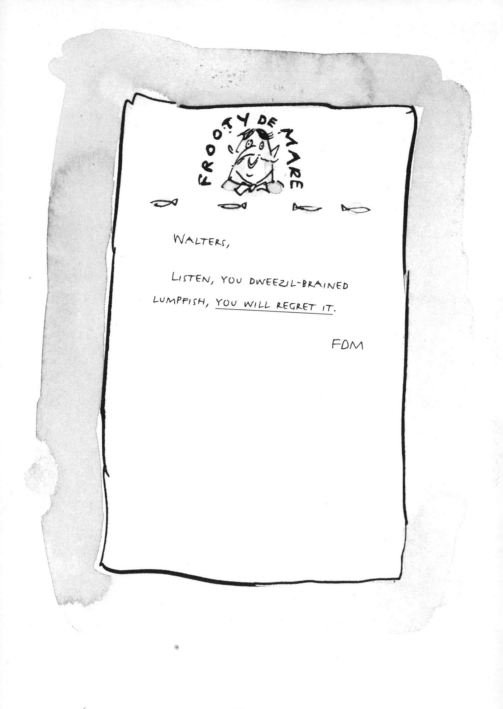

WALTERS,

LISTEN, YOU DWEEZIL-BRAINED
LUMPFISH, <u>YOU WILL REGRET IT.</u>

FDM

CHAPTER
18

BY THE TIME HER MOTHER HAD crossed Lake Balkhash, 298 miles from the Chinese border, Thora had filled almost one half of the blank book given to her by Mr. Walters. Reviewing it revealed that Thora could walk, talk, somersault, say hello in twelve languages, and hoist a sail. Mr. Walters had taught her to play cricket. He had taught her how to ride a bicycle. He had even taught her how to cook. Before her eighth birthday, Thora could make Thai chicken satay, Ukrainian pirogi, and Italian spaghetti. Mr. Walters was a good coach and a reliable human guardian. He treated Thora like his own grandchild. In time he couldn't imagine life without her. Sometimes he had to go off to attend to what he called his "kitchen of life." But he always came back. Halla and Thora were always happy to see him.

And as he grew older, it was Thora who used her two young legs to walk to the shops to buy the milk, her scales

As the Sea Shrew said
If you produce a child
~~Half~~ of the land and sea
It ~~will~~ have to live in both
In order to be Free

TEN YEARS AT SEA! TEN YEARS ON LAND!
BETWEEN TWO WORLDS THIS GIRL MUST STAND!

Prophecies are always a little
confusing but it doesn't take a
~~brain surgeon~~ circumpolar navigation
officer to understand that I had
to get myself to land.

What better place to go than to
where Daddy grew up?

well hidden beneath her Halla-Skin and her purple feet covered by windsurfing slippers. It was Thora who collected Halla's prizes on behalf of her mother, and Thora who reminded everybody that after the next major swim, they would have to head back to Grimli because their ten years between worlds was almost up.

CHAPTER
19

ON THE EVE OF THORA'S TENTH birthday, Thora, Halla, Mr. Walters, and Cosmo set sail for Grimli. Passage through the Panama Canal and the Pacific and Indian Oceans was rough. The *Loki* took a beating and, though they made good time, the vessel was leaking by the time they reached the Rock.

Mr. Walters was pitched into gloom. They would have to find a place to stay until the boat was repaired. "I hadn't planned for this," he fussed. "Life can be so trying sometimes."

Thora was gloomy too, but for different reasons. The Rock, situated about five miles from town, was to be Halla's new home. "You've got to be kidding. . . . You're actually going to live *here*?"

"Yes," sang Halla. "Isn't it wonderful?" She greeted it like an old friend. She seemed familiar with every fissure. It was "full of potential," she said, and had a number of "terrific lounging opportunities."

Thora did not think the Rock was wonderful. *At all.*

It was the size of a squash court, though oblong in shape and hedged with pebbly bits and tooth-shaped rocks. Flattish. A sloping ramp at the north end was furred with mosses, lichens, seaweed. It just sat there doing nothing. It was just a boring old rock.

To Mr. Walters, it looked like a Stilton cheese after a large dinner party.

But Cosmo seemed to sense that it was alive with hundreds of tiny sea creatures. He fanned his tail and held his beak up to catch the fishy smells.

"Look," said Halla. "I know it's not exactly luxury accommodation. But I'm a mermaid, remember? I don't need roofs and beds and hair dryers and television sets. The wind will be my hair dryer and the sea will be my fridge. Besides, I can come to visit you in the *Loki* once you're all set up."

"It doesn't even have a toilet," said Thora, ignoring her mother.

They all surveyed the Rock in silence.

"Well," said Mr. Walters, turning to Halla. "Here's a plus. The view is excellent. You can see the Grimli pier from here."

"Exactly," said Halla. She began unpacking her bags. "What are you all waiting for? We have a birthday to celebrate!"

They all set to scrubbing away the slime with pumice stones. Halla braided the slippery bits of seaweed and shook out an old red-and-white-checkered tablecloth. Then she produced Thora's favorite—pineapple sea-foam angel cake.

It was a bittersweet occasion.

Mr. Walters smoked his cigar and stared at a distant point on the sea.

Cosmo scratched at the lichen with his three-pointed toes.

Halla busied herself cleaning up and settling in.

Thora tried to imagine the life that lay ahead.

Soon Mr. Walters and Cosmo sailed off in the *Loki* to make arrangements. In a few hours, they would collect Thora and take her to Grimli to begin her life on land.

CHAPTER

20

MOTHER AND DAUGHTER WERE ALONE TOGETHER.

With a comb made of abalone shell, Halla brushed
Thora's hair as she had done since Thora was small. She
fastened it in a ponytail at the top of her head. "You've got
to hide your blowhole. Humans don't spout water out of
the tops of their heads, and they'll find it strange."

She handed Thora a bag containing two wet suits and several pairs of wind-surfing slippers. "The scales on your legs are beautiful, but sadly, humans find them ugly. You just can't risk it. I've heard of a mermaid who was de-scaled by humans. She died. Be very, very careful."

"Mom, I know all of this."

Halla persevered. "Keep your scales covered at all times. As for the puddles from your blowhole, they'll assume you've wet yourself. Humans always take the silliest position on this sort of thing. Always carry something to mop up. And keep your feet hidden. Humans aren't very open-minded when it comes to purple feet."

Finally she pushed the tea chest toward Thora.

"Humans love presents. Always take a present when you visit. Afterward write a thank-you note. People consider you quite rude otherwise. Be very careful about who you get to know. If you run into any sort of trouble, go to the movies. Your father once worked at the Allbent Cinema. Never forget that the sisters saved your life when you were one week old." She paused and looked over to the Grimli skyline. "I've always wanted to meet those sisters," she said. "Maybe you could tell them that for me."

Thora nodded. "Anything else?"

"Most things that human beings do are a mystery," said Halla.

Thora grabbed her book and flipped it open to the page where she kept an ongoing list of mysterious human activities. "Snorkeling, crying, raffles, cheerleading, golf, fishing," she read off.

"I'm sure you'll be adding to your list," said Halla. "Just listen to Mr. Walters. He knows the ropes."

At that moment Mr. Walters appeared in their old canoe. He climbed out with an "Oof." Over his white pullover, he wore a bright orange life jacket. He removed a hanky from his pocket and dabbed his forehead. "Hey, ho," he said, tipping his bowler hat. "We'll have to spend the night at a motel."

Halla nodded and continued speaking to her daughter. "I'll be here on the Rock until you two set yourselves up in the *Loki*. Time alone on land with Mr. Walters will help you get your bearings. I can swim in for good-night kisses. But best that we wait until after dark. We mustn't be seen." They held hands and together looked out at the Grimli skyline.

"I wonder what causes that orange glow," said Thora.

Halla shrugged. "It's new," she said. "It wasn't there when you were a baby."

Mr. Walters jumped back into the canoe and Thora followed. Mr. Walters then pushed off with the end of his paddle. "Cheerio," he said to Halla. "You take a little break now. You deserve it."

"It will be heavenly just to sit and do nothing," said Halla. "Now don't look so sad, Thora. This is your time now. Your chance to find your feet. Make the most of it!"

CHAPTER
21

THE SEA WAS CHOPPY, THE SURFACE spread with restless peaks—like a birthday cake iced in a hurry.

Dusk was sifting down. Across the water, half a mile away, the town threw off an orange glow.

"It's like somebody threw iodine at the sky," observed Thora.

"An abomination," agreed Mr. Walters. "Frooty's neon signs should be banned."

It was Thora's idea that they return the *Loki* to Grimli. She wanted to explore the town where her father had grown up and to meet the sisters who had saved her life when she was a baby. Mr. Walters did not love the idea of returning to this town, mainly on account of Frooty de Mare. He had not mentioned Frooty's letters to Halla or to Thora as he had not wanted to worry them. The lease belonged to him, fair and square. Even so, when Frooty heard about the return of the *Loki*, he was bound to pay them a visit.

As always, the very thought of Frooty's name made Mr. Walters think of wrecking balls.

With the Blue Bell Bed and Breakfast no longer in existence, they would have to walk through town to the cinema, where he would introduce Thora to the Greenberg sisters and ask them to recommend a nice place to stay.

He rather looked forward to seeing the three women again. Especially Flossie.

They entered the old Grimli harbor and glided past the bruised and battered *Loki* and toward the shore. Mr. Walters was comforted by the fact that, despite all the changes to the town, the harbor looked much as it had when they'd left it ten years ago.

Thora broke the silence with a shout. "Look up there!"

Sitting on an old oil drum at the end of the pier was a boy of about twelve. They passed under him so closely that they could see the mosquito bites on his arms.

Thora waved. "Ahoy!"

He was waiting with his dog and his bicycle on the jetty when they docked the boat. He wore a dirty yellow T-shirt, and his ears stuck out.

"Hello. I'm Ricky. Welcome to Grimli. Population four thousand."

"Four thousand plus three," said Thora. Then under

her breath: "Four if you include Mother."

"You moving to town then?"

"Until I find my feet," said Thora.

He looked down. "Have you lost them or something?"

"No," she said, stepping into her wind-surf slippers. "It's a figurine of speech."

"Christmas!" he hollered. "What's wrong with you? Your toes are bright *purple!*"

"Just a touch of poor circulation," said Thora. "It runs in the family." She looked hard at Ricky. "Hey, are you like one of those boys in Tangiers who greet the ferry and try to sell a night in their uncle's hotel?"

"Nope," he said. "I don't have an uncle and he don't have a hotel! But I could sell you a ride on my bike to the Tooty Frooty."

"We're not staying there," clipped Mr. Walters.

"Really?" drawled Ricky. "Everyone else does. Not much else going on here, except for the casino and the games room. Where have you come from?"

"The Rock," answered Thora,

leaping out of the canoe. She held out her hand for the dog to sniff.

"You're kidding!" He whistled.

"Before that we were living between worlds. Ten years at sea and not one pirate ship!"

Ricky gave Thora a curious look. "How did you do it? The Rock, I mean. What was it like? And in a canoe!" He looked impressed. "Tiny Stevens and me are gonna get there someday soon."

His dog panted and wagged its mangy tail.

Mr. Walters frowned. "No," he said. "It's a dreadful place. You don't want to go there. Teeming with leeches and jelly-fish. Extremely dangerous. I'm surprised they haven't posted up warning signs."

"Oh, they have," said Ricky. "But the winds take them down. There's a rip that runs alongside. The coast guard is always talking about it. We learned about it in school. Once a fisherman got lost near there. People around here stay clear of the Rock." He looked out across the harbor. "That's why I wanna go."

"I would advise that you listen to the coast guard and to your teachers and stay away." Mr. Walters tipped his bowler hat at the boy and went off to have a word with the har-bormaster.

"There's nicer places to visit, anyway," said Thora. She

sat down on the pier to put on her wind-surf slippers. "More constantinopalising places."

Abruptly a white truck pulled up at the pier. A very fat man jumped out. He was stuffing a hamburger into his mouth and looking around.

"Oh-oh," said the boy, spinning around. "I gotta go."

"Where have you been, you little brat?" shouted the man. Bits of hamburger meat and lettuce were stuck to his chin. "I told you to come right back on home after you bought the lottery tickets."

Ricky waved the tickets at Thora and, groaning, ran toward the truck. "Coming, coming, coming!"

The man pushed him roughly into the backseat of the truck. Then he reached through the open window into the front seat and pulled out a can of pop. When he had polished it off, he tossed the empty can at Ricky, wiped his mouth with a hairy tattooed forearm, and returned for the bicycle.

"What in a dog's breakfast are *you* looking at?" he said to Thora.

"I'm not looking," she replied primly. "I'm staring."

"Well, stop it then." He lifted the bike up over his head and tossed it into the trailer. There was a crash as metal hit metal.

"Hey," cried Thora. "Don't forget your dog!"

The man jumped into the truck and drove off. The dog barked and ran after them.

"What was that all about?" asked Mr. Walters.

"Someone who got up on the wrong side of the Mid-Atlantic Ridge." Thora shrugged. "But Ricky seemed all right."

CHAPTER
22

THEY HEADED OFF ACROSS THE LENGTHENING shadows of the dockyard, through a maze of peeling boathouses, spiderwebs, and old rotting fish and rope smells.

Thora could hear the pitter-patter of mouse feet in the scaffoldings, the spongy clop of Mr. Walters's Blundstone boots.

They emerged from the dockyard onto Grimli's main street just as the sun was dropping over the water. Mr. Walters pointed. The Allbent Cinema was at the end of the next block.

Thora took a deep breath and hugged her bag close.

She was too excited to see Halla wave her good night from the Rock, now a dot on the pink water.

She took no notice of the people staring, or of Mr. Walters, who hurried along ahead.

This was the street her father had walked.

This was the bakery where he had bought his cream doughnuts.

Here was the fish shop, the greengrocer, the butcher.

There was the cinema, where he'd had a job.

Some of these people might have even *spoken* to him.

Of course, she wasn't entirely sure about all of this, but she was quite sure that her father had liked cream doughnuts. Most people did!

Soon they came to a rather old-fashioned Mediterranean-style building with an orange roof. The Allbent Cinema.

"It looks exactly like the ravioli factory in Mantua," enthused Thora, feeling hungry all of a sudden.

Mr. Walters knocked, and eventually a girl with mousy brown hair wearing a long black mohair sweater came to the door. She informed them that the sisters were away at the Venice Film Festival and would not be back for another month or so.

Mr. Walters was crestfallen. "Can you suggest a good bed and breakfast?"

"No, there aren't any. On the edge of town, a mile or so away, you'll find the Viking Motor Inn. Otherwise, the only place to stay is across the street." She made a face. "At the Tooty Frooty. It's a little seedy these days, but it depends whether you care about that sort of thing."

Mr. Walters and Thora crossed the street for a look. Mr. Walters already knew what they would find.

It was one of those places that you almost always find in a seaside town. A restaurant hotel built to resemble a boat.

This boat looked like it would capsize instantly in the water, Thora thought as she examined its mauve and gold hull.

The orange sign read:

TOOTY FROOTY
HOTEL & SEAFOOD EMPORIUM

Directly above the sign, a cartoon mermaid flicked her neon tail.

So *this* was what gave the town its mysterious glow.

"Tasteless," remarked Mr. Walters.

"Revulsive," agreed Thora, heading up the steps. "But that's not a good reason not to stay here while we repair the *Loki*."

A large slit on the side of the hull blew a hot blast of onion-ring air right into Thora's face. Her ponytail stood straight up.

"A vile establishment," said Mr. Walters. "As you shall see."

He didn't try to stop Thora. He was accustomed to her investigations. He lit a cigar and found a shadow to stand in.

CHAPTER
23

AT THE TOP OF THE STEPS, she pushed through the door. A large, yellowing poster board greeted her.

Congratulations
to
FROOTY DE MARE
for continued service excellence
THE MAYOR'S
OFFICE · GRIMLI

At the end of a small, mirror-lined corridor, she passed into a crowded, smoky room.

A party?

Nobody greeted her. Nobody even looked her way.

They all stood staring at the whirring, buzzing, glowing, pulsing, ringing television screens on the walls.

She tapped a man on the shoulder. "Excuse me, sir. What are you doing?" she asked.

It was the grumpy man she'd seen at the pier.

"Losing all my money," he grunted. "Shoo."

"Shoofly to you, too," said Thora indignantly.

She wandered up a little set of stairs, across a small wooden bridge. Down more stairs and into a large, empty restaurant with floor-to-ceiling glass windows and a good view of the twinkling harbor. On one side was a marine display that included a stuffed mermaid.

"How odd," said Thora. Lining the back wall was an enormous aquarium. *Glug glug glug.* Where were the fish? The water was too murky to tell. The specials of the day were announced on a large sandwich board.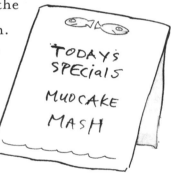

There was a desk. On the desk, a bell. Thora rang the bell. It made a jangling noise.

"Hold your horses," came a voice.

"I don't have any horses," Thora shouted. "Only a peacock named Cosmo."

A red-haired woman appeared. She wore a sparkly tiara and a tight, parrot green top. A badge said MADGE. "What can I do for you?" she asked.

"Any rooms for sale? A small room will do, preferably with a bunk bed each for me and my guardian and a bottom drawer for Cosmo here to sleep in."

"Sorry, I'm not the person to speak to about rooms. You'll have to go back to the main entrance and turn left to get to the reception desk for the hotel. Look, save yourself the effort. There's an elevator over there." She pointed.

"Does it work?"

"Should do."

"Hah, then it's ripe to break down. I like my elevators out of service. Then you take the stairs and no worries, mate. We stayed once at one of the finest hotels in England. The Savoy Cabbage was the name. I got stuck in the elevator. Guess who was stuck with me?"

Madge shrugged. "Old Liz?"

Thora guffawed. "You mean Her Majesty? Are you kidding? The queen doesn't take elevators." Thora leaned forward. "It was another kind of queen. The queen of the lawn-bowling circuit: Doris Danforth!"

Madge looked bored. "Look, let me show you where the reception desk is." They passed close by the display of fake sea creatures and then headed up the stairs.

When they reached the reception desk, Thora paused. "What's that terrible racket?"

Madge held up her index finger. "Shh."

Behind the reception desk was a gold door marked "CEO, Tooty Frooty Enterprises." The voice that stormed out from behind it was angry.

"After all I've done for this two-bit town—you'd think you'd help me out on this one, you big meany!"

"Who's that?" asked Thora.

"The CEO of this dump," said Madge through tight lips. "Frooty de Mare."

"Dump?" said Thora looking around. "I don't see any rubbish."

Madge snorted. "Let me tell you, there's plenty of *that*." She located the hotel register and opened it. "Between you and me, Frooty's losing his marbles."

Suddenly the door opened and Frooty stomped out, looking for his eyeglasses. When he put them on, he glared at Thora.

"Who is this? What is going on?" he asked.

"I was just admiring the view," said Thora pleasantly. "But I must ask you . . . why a stuffed mermaid when you could have a real one?"

"Listen, missy, if there was a real one to have, I'd have her," he said. He stomped back into his office and slammed the door. Thora shivered.

"Between you and me, Madge, I gotta get going. Too many fake sea creatures for my taste."

CHAPTER
24

FOR ONE MONTH, MR. WALTERS AND Thora lived at the Viking Motor Inn on the edge of town. Mr. Walters did not want Frooty de Mare sniffing around asking questions, and so he arranged for the *Loki* to be transported to a rented hangar near the airport. During the days, he and Thora worked very hard on repairs to the *Loki*. Ten years of round-the-world sailing had taken its toll. The hull was so encrusted with barnacles that it resembled a tortoise shell. The cabin bore the lashings of the wind and waves. Paint hung from the sides like the curling bark on a eucalyptus tree.

In the evenings, Thora met her mother at the end of the pier to give her updates on their progress and to kiss her good night. It felt very odd to see Halla swim off into the darkness. But it was exciting to creep through the town in darkness. She was very careful not to be seen.

Before bedtime, they read more books: Mr. Walters,

Major General Sir John Hackett's World War III, and Thora, *The Complete Treasury of Falkland Islands Fables*.

They finished their repairs just as summer gave way to autumn and the air turned chilly.

Mr. Walters peeled away the rug in the center of the main cabin. It was a beautiful Turkish wool carpet with patterns of red and yellow diamonds and a gold fringe. It had been awarded to Halla after she swam the Bosphorus.

They had covered the pizza-sized hole on the floor of the *Loki* with Plexiglas to keep out the chill of the sea. To open it, Thora simply had to slide back the glass. To take the edge off Thora's homesickness for the sea, they had also installed a five-hundred-watt sea lamp from a swimming pool in Shreveport, Louisiana, which produced a cone of light that illuminated sea creatures in the sea below.

The hull sported a new coat of glossy white paint. The cabin had been enlarged. The roof retiled. When they transported the *Loki* back to the harbor, it looked like a brand-new boat.

"All it needs now," said Thora, "are a few fenimen touches."

"You mean feminine," Mr. Walters corrected.

"Sure," said Thora.

"I'll leave that up to you and your mother," said Mr. Walters.

Neither he nor Halla knew what living on land would do to Thora. He was pleased to see that so far Thora was prospering. Even if she wobbled over certain words.

Halla arrived to celebrate their return to the *Loki*. They had a party and broke a bottle of raspberry cordial over the stern. "To the *Loki*!" they all shouted merrily.

The mood was dampened by the arrival of a telegram bearing sad news. That morning Mr. Walters's dear brother, who was a sheep farmer, had died in Port Desire, Argentina. His brother's son hoped very much that Mr. Walters might be able to attend the funeral.

He was not so sure that he wanted to leave Thora by herself, but Halla pointed out that she would be coming around each night to share a cup of tea and to tuck Thora into bed.

"The sisters will be back soon," Thora added. "I can always visit them if I feel lonely."

"And I'm sure that Thora will soon make some friends," said Halla. "You mustn't worry."

Mr. Walters put a new chain belt around Thora's waist, onto which he had welded five of Halla's medals.

"This is for good luck," he said, and then from his suit pocket he produced a fat cod-skin wallet stuffed with traveler's checks.

"Make sure you get a good exchange rate."

"Righty-o," said Thora.

Mr. Walters shook both of Halla's hands and then he kissed the top of Thora's head. There was a sudden hiss. He jumped back. A jet of water sprayed out and drenched them all. Thora pulled her hair up and refastened her ponytail scrunchie. They both laughed. A mermaid's farewell never failed to take Mr. Walters by surprise.

"Well, I'll be off," he said. "There will be some family business to settle after the funeral, but I'll be in touch."

"The time will pass faster than a shoal of fish," said Halla.

"Give it all you've got!" said Thora, giving him the thumbs-up signal. Her thumbs didn't seem to be working properly and her words sounded a little flat, so she added, "Break a leg! Write if you remember!"

Mr. Walters turned to Cosmo. "Watch out for that beak of yours," he said. "No scratching the good wooden floors." Then he turned back to Thora. "He's good company," he said. "Even if he *is* a little vain."

Thora watched Mr. Walters climb into his taxicab. "Don't be sad, big fellow," she said to Cosmo. "Mr. Walters will be back soon." She did a cartwheel and landed with a *smuch!* on her bottom in a small puddle of water. "Ouch," she said a little sadly.

"Everything is changing very fast," said Halla. She gave her daughter a shimmery hug. "You'll feel better after a good night's sleep."

CHAPTER

25

THE HARDWARE STORE WAS DARK AND cramped and smelled of wood bits and gear chains.

"What a cozy place," Thora murmured, running her finger along the dusty shelves.

In the Paint section she spun the color wheel, settling for the colors that made her mouth water: three liters of Shrimp Pink, five liters of Quay-Lime Green.

In Housewares she selected an angel food cake tin, a set of blue tin cups, and an oven mitt in the shape of a flounder.

The woman behind the counter reached for Thora's basket. "Will that be all?"

Thora scratched her chin thoughtfully. "I'm doing a little *inner decorating*," she said. "Could you add a few walls of that wallpaper to my bill, please? The furry green variety?"

"That's not wallpaper," said the woman. "It's indoor-outdoor carpet."

"Fine," said Thora coolly. "I'll take thirty square feet." She was not entirely sure what a square foot was, but luckily the woman seemed to know.

"Oh, and one last thing! I'd like a dozen pink flamingos. The plastic ones, of course. Real flamingos are impractical birds for these climes, but a dozen plastic flamingos will do the trick. Now what is the rate of exchange for a traveler's check?"

She returned to the pier and set up the pink flamingos in a line on the deck of the *Loki*.

She rolled out the carpet and hung it on her bedroom wall.

Then with the pink and quay-lime paint she made up a sign and nailed it onto the cabin door:

TRESPASSERS WILL BE PROSTLETYSED

She was having so much fun that she made another sign:

MAID, PLEASE MAKE UP MY ROOM

And another:

NO LOITERING, SPITTING, RUNNING ON DECK

"A girl can't run on empty," she said to Cosmo. She reached for a large glass bowl and whipped up a batter of egg whites, sugar, cream of tartar, and flour and poured it into

91

her new angel food cake tin. Soon the old smell of Mr. Walters's cigar smoke and Irish Spring aftershave were mingling with the sweet smell of baking cake. It was 9:00 P.M. She switched on the sea lamp and slid back the Plexiglas cover. Her timing was excellent. Halla surfaced in the *Loki* just as the kettle began to sing "Oh Susannah." Halla propped herself up on her elbows, eyes wide. "What's wrong with those flamingos out on the deck?" she asked. "Not even a wing salute!"

Thora laughed. "They're fake," she said. "I just liked the color!"

Halla looked a little relieved. Flamingos did not generally

like to feed on mermaids, but they had been known to try.

Thora passed her mother a cup of Russian Caravan tea (with a good dash of warm milk and three lumps of brown sugar). They drank in companionable silence.

Then Halla kissed her and prepared to depart for the Rock.

"When the paint dries, I'll have to give some very serious consideration to the furniture and inner decorations. Really, Mother, I have *barely scratched* the surface."

CHAPTER
26

THORA WAS AWOKEN VERY EARLY THE next morning by a tremendous vibrating noise in the sky.

"Jeepers!" she cried, leaping out of bed. "What's all this kakka-phony? Oh, look, Cosmo! It's an arrow-plane!"

Cosmo burrowed his head into the breadbox and whimpered.

Thora opened the door and rushed out onto the pier. She had seen a number of aircraft in her time, but never one with flashing wings and gold pontoons.

For a moment, she wondered if it wasn't some overgrown parrot on his way to the Amazon. But then the wings dipped, and as the plane turned she could see the cockpit and a number of white faces pressed against the glass.

Trailing after it, like a long ribbon, was a banner.

FROOTY DE MARE'S CELEBRATION CONTINUES: SAMPLE OUR WORLD-FAMOUS SHRIMP PIE & ONION RINGS!

The plane did a somersault and headed back the way it had come.

There is something about an airplane that makes one look up and wave. With the exception of a fisherman hauling his nets into his boat, Thora was quite alone on the pier that morning. She waved at the swooping plane. Somebody in the cockpit waved back.

"I say, mister," she shouted to the fisherman, "isn't it a wonderful show?"

The old fisherman shook his head and removed his earplugs. Thora repeated herself. The fisherman flicked his hand. "Nah, it's a nuisance. Pure noise pollution. That's why I wear these."

"Cosmo is like you," said Thora. "But I *love* the noise. It reminds me of the helicopters in Marrakech! They were always buzzing around us when my mother went to open their Roman swimming pool. Very exhilarating!"

The fisherman made a face. "Don't be fooled," he said, and disappeared into the cabin of his boat.

The plane performed a few more tricks before landing in the harbor. Out of nowhere, an official-looking boat with quivering antennae sprinted across the water and stopped beside the plane. The door of the plane opened. A ladder dropped down. Led by a bad-tempered man in a black leather coat, six people climbed out.

The coast guard delivered them to the pier. The man stepped onto it and yelled at his sons to help their mother with her bags. "I have people to meet. Places to go! Get a move on!"

Thora would have known that voice anywhere. It sounded like rust and grit and wet sand.

The man with the silly name: Frooty de Mare.

He rushed off, leaving three hulking sons with shaved heads and baggy jeans, a short, round fusspot woman in a yellow scarf, and finally, lagging behind the group, with a faraway look in her eyes, a much younger girl.

She had wonderful dark curly hair and wore an old-fashioned red tartan kilt. She was no more than thirty feet from Thora.

"Hey, girl in the kilt!" yelled Thora. "Over here!"

CHAPTER
27

HOLLY WAS ABOUT TO FOLLOW HER mother onto the de Mares' very large family cabin cruiser when Thora stuck out her tongue.

It was the longest tongue Holly had ever seen. And above the tongue were the greenest green eyes Holly had ever seen.

She was alarmed by the *clang* of the medals around the girl's waist and by the hair that hung in her face and by the weird black rubber suit she wore.

Suddenly the tongue snapped back into the girl's mouth and she rubbed her tummy. "Yum," she said. "It's rude to stare. Didn't your mother teach you that? Mine did, before she swam out between the icebergs in Hudson Bay. I was staring at a polar bear at the time."

Holly's bow lips formed a perfect O.

"Excellent way to trap a fly," said Thora.

Holly quickly covered her mouth.

"You see," continued Thora, "when the polar bear saw me staring, he charged at me and would have eaten me if I hadn't dropped to the ground and pretended to be dead. Polar bears, *Ursus maritimus*, are flesh-eating mammals. They prefer girls with long black curly hair and tartan kilts. But there are so few of them up north that they have to settle for skinny girls with brown hair and itchy elbows." She scratched her elbows, first one and then the other.

Holly looked around. "There aren't any polar bears in Grimli."

"I believe not," Thora assured her. "Sadly. And anyway, polar bears prefer tough meat to tender. So you are automatically disqualified."

Holly stiffened.

To make her smile, Thora began a dance, a little Highland fling that Mr. Walters had taught her. "Of course, it isn't the same without bagpipes. If I could borrow your bladder for a second, we could straighten that out."

"My *bladder*?"

"Bagpipes are made out of bladders. Mr. Walters is one-quarter Scottish. He told me all about it. The old Scotsmen were very good inventors. Take your kilt, for instance. They invented plaid. They liked it so much that the men wore plaid skirts to fight in the war! Imagine! Brave soldiers in skirts! What a funny place."

"Who's Mr. Walters?"

"My human guardian angle."

Holly looked puzzled.

"Anyway," continued Thora, "in Scotland my mother swam Loch Ness. She had to drop out because of the Loch Ness monster. But they were on very good terms by the time we left. We even had Nessie aboard for scones and a drop of warming Scotch whisky."

Holly frowned.

"Oh, dear," said Thora, "I've upset you again. Maybe we can start again over a nice cup of Russian Caravan tea." She jumped from the pier onto the *Loki*. "Come on in. You can listen to our kettle sing. Do you like the tune 'Oh Susannah'?"

"I don't drink tea," said Holly, following her onto the deck and into the cabin. "It contains tannic acid and other harmful additives."

"Then how about some octopus cheeks? I believe we have a few leftovers. I can reheat them in a jiffy." She began to light the gas stove with a long wooden match.

"I'm not allowed to play with matches."

"Play? We're not *playing*." Thora laughed.

"That's my mother calling me," said Holly suddenly. "I have to go, right now!"

"No worries," said Thora brightly. "There's a luxury

toilet thataway! It even has an electric velvet seat cover to warm your bottom."

Holly blushed. "That's not at all what I meant," she said, reaching for the door. "My mother is wondering where I am. Good-bye . . ."

"Drop by for tea anytime!" shouted Thora. "We were only just getting warmed up!"

CHAPTER
28

FROOTY RUSHED DOWN THE PIER TOWARD his office. He did not even notice that the *Loki* now occupied the berth he had once been so desperate to get hold of. His mind was too full of his latest great idea.

It had come to him in the dead of night. That's how it usually worked with geniuses. He'd been thinking his usual thoughts about how to get rid of the Greenberg sisters. How he hated those old hags! He'd had his sons unleash rats in the aisles of the theater and tried to have it declared a public health hazard. He'd tried to burn them down, freeze them up, smoke them out. But so far, nothing had worked. People kept going to their dingy old cinema to see their boring arty-farty movies. He just didn't get it.

Anyway, as he tossed and turned in the super-king-sized, vibrating bed that he shared with Mrs. de Mare, the idea came to him.

If you can't get rid of them, beat them at their own game!

He'd open up his own cinema and steal their customers!

It had taken him only six weeks to convert an old waterfront bed and breakfast into a triplex cinema that would seat three hundred people. When it opened in one month's time, he would throw a big party and invite the whole town—except for the Greenberg sisters, of course. Plans were well under way for a parade, a pancake breakfast, and a hammer-throwing contest.

He just needed a name.

CHAPTER
29

A WEEK OR SO AFTER HOLLY'S visit, Thora was mending cobwebs on the ceiling of her little cabin when her mother dropped by for a quick visit.

"Thora, these cobwebs can wait. Why don't you go and see if the sisters have returned from Venice?"

"But it's raining, Mother," said Thora. Cold, fat drops from a stone-colored sky.

"Since when has a little bit of water put you off your game?"

Thora climbed down the ladder and dried her hands on the curtains. "You're right. The sisters should be back by now."

She tied a flowered plastic rain bonnet onto Cosmo's head, kissed her mother's pumpkin pie–scented head good-bye, and headed off with Cosmo to the cinema.

To Thora's surprise, the streets were deserted.

"In India they would be out celebrating the rain!" She

performed a little dance she had been taught in Calcutta during a monsoon. "Maybe the residents of Grimli just don't appreciate water the way we do."

A sign in the window of Gulli's Goodies took Thora by surprise:

CLOSED DUE TO FLOODING

"How unfortunate," she said. "Cupcakes taste best in the rain."

The Tooty Frooty gave off a lonely air. Even the builders on Frooty's latest construction site were silent.

Thora began to whistle a song she had learned from the Xanti in the Amazon. It was a very sad tune in a minor key about a girl who had lost her grandfather and was weeping by the river where he'd been eaten by an anaconda.

The sad tune and the pelting rain all around her made her feel lonely for Mr. Walters. His crinkly, triangular eyes. His cooked breakfasts.

She hoped that Mr. Walters was safe from anacondas.

She stood for a minute staring at the water between the gap in the buildings. The color of the sea was always changing. It was always worth a look. Today it was gray, gray, gray.

Except for a bright bit of red flashing between the waves.

Thora had excellent vision. But she could hardly believe her eyes when she saw that the flashing red bit in the water was in fact her very own canoe!

What was it doing out at sea? Surely Mr. Walters hadn't returned to Grimli without telling them!

She stared hard.

The person in the boat was moving around so much it was hard to focus. When she did, she saw thin arms and sticky-outy ears. "The boy from the pier!" she said to Cosmo. "Ricky!"

A gust of wind caught her ponytail. She turned around and saw a police car speed by. Then came the sound of an ambulance and several people shouting and running toward the beach. He must be in danger!

CHAPTER
30

BY THE TIME THORA GOT TO the beach, a crowd had formed. A few people glanced her way, but nobody spoke to her. They were all staring and pointing out to sea at the boy in the red canoe. Everyone was talking at once.

"He stole the boat from the dockyards."

"He's *always* running away."

"He's caught in a rip."

"Why is the coast guard taking so long?"

"I don't think he's even wearing a life jacket."

Then a pale woman fell to her knees and began to sob. "He doesn't know how to swim! Somebody, please save him!"

"Come on, Cosmo," whispered Thora. "We don't have a lot of time."

Thora headed down the beach. When she was out of sight of the crowd, she slipped into the heaving water. Up close it looked less gray and more green, the color of the sage leaves that Mr. Walters liked to sprinkle on his rice pudding. She dived down deep and began to swim.

The strength of the rip surprised her. She was breathing hard when she surfaced, remembering the massive rips in the sea at Bilgola Beach in Sydney. Halla had taught her how to swim diagonally against the pulling water. She did now as she approached the canoe from the ocean side, careful to keep her head low so that the people on shore couldn't see her.

She steered the canoe at an angle and turned it so that it faced the shore.

Ricky stopped paddling and looked over his shoulder. The wind had messed up his hair, his cheeks were red, and he had a slightly wild look in his dark eyes. "What are *you* doing here?" he shouted above the wind. She steadied the boat and continued pushing.

"You're caught in the rip," said Thora.

"No," said the boy. "Let me go."

"If I let you go, you'll be drawn out to sea."

"Let go!" he shouted. "I don't want to go home!"

"Righty-o," said Thora, letting go.

The canoe spun around like a bottle and shot off. Ricky lost his balance and almost toppled out of the boat. "Help!"

She swam after him. "You changed your mind yet?"

"Yes!" he cried. Immediately he looked as if he regretted it.

"I'll help you on one condition. Don't mention I helped."

"Why?"

"I'm undercover."

The sea was pulling him away fast. "All right, all right," he managed. "Whatever you say."

Thora righted the boat and guided it out of the rip. The muscular tug of the water against them was using up Thora's strength. She wished Halla were there to help.

Like an echo of her thoughts, there was a *click*.

The wind died. A soft *whoosh*.

Thora felt a soft, warm breeze at her back. The boat glided along effortlessly. Thora removed her fingertips. It continued for shore as if propelled by its own invisible engine.

"Thanks, Mother," whispered Thora to the waves.

CHAPTER
31

BEFORE THEY OPENED THE ALLBENT CINEMA, Lottie, Flossie and Dottie Greenberg were three glamorous sisters with an interest in clothes and movie stars. Here is a photo of them when they were young:

Lottie was the brain. Flossie, the feisty one. Dottie, the dreamer. They were stylish and vivacious, and worked part-time jobs in town: Flossie in the bakery where she iced cupcakes and decorated the gingerbread men in ice-hockey and baseball uniforms; Lottie as a teller at the bank; Dottie as a seamstress and dressmaker.

Every few years they traveled by passenger ship to Europe and returned wearing the latest European fashions: silk scarves, oversized sunglasses, animal-patterned handbags, odd little boots lined with poodle fur. There clung to them an air of otherworldliness that both repelled and fascinated, like strong perfume. It might not be your taste, but you got used to it after a while.

The sisters thought nothing of changing their hair color, piercing their ears, or sunbathing on the pier in skimpy two-piece bathing suits. They took long walks together, flew kites in the park, kept a pet iguana on the radiator in their sun room, and even roller-skated to work when they felt like it.

The sisters had boyfriends, although never anything very serious. They always intended to get married but somehow never got around to it. Sisters can be lazy about certain things when they have each other to fall back on. They liked their life just the way it was.

It was on a trip to Venice that the sisters fell in love for the first time—with the movies. But Grimli had no cinema. When the old Lutheran church was struck by lightning and the minister moved his congregation across town, the sisters pooled their cash and bought the building. They named it the Allbent because the lightning had hit the church steeple and the building leaned a little to the left.

A film screen from Hollywood was installed. A projector was purchased from a traveling spiritualist in a caravan. Old plush velvet seats were bought at auction.

On the cinema's opening night, every seat was sold, and within a month, the Allbent was the most popular place in town. If you listened, you could hear the mysterious sounds of the cinema from any point in town.

On Mondays, the sound of people swooning. On Tuesdays, laughter. Wednesdays, weeping. Thursdays, cries of fright and horror. Fridays, sighs. And on the weekends, a little bit of everything. It was as if the projector were capable of giving life and color to every emotion experienced by the inhabitants of the small seaside town. For a period of about five years, the cinema sisters were the town's darlings.

It was Dottie's announcement that she was going to have a baby that changed everything. While the unexpected news was received by the sisters with surprising calm, the people of Grimli were a little less accepting. Attendance at the cinema fell. Nevertheless, the sisters persevered. The child was born and grew up in the flickering lights of the cinema aisles and seats. Though it was an unusual childhood, the theater was a happy environment. He had everything he needed.

On this rainy day, when everything in town was either flooded or closed, a welcoming light shone through the steamed-up stained-glass windows of the Allbent Cinema.

Thora opened the door and took a deep breath of the buttery-smelling lobby air.

On the walls were posters of famous old movie stars: Greta Garbo, Clark Gable, Vivien Leigh. There were also posters of more recent movie stars, but in color they were not nearly as glamorous.

The girl behind the counter in the black mohair sweater was painting her nails purple. "Movie starts in three minutes," she said without looking up.

"I came to meet the Greenberg sisters. I would have come sooner, but I've been busier than an octopus on a construction site."

"The Greenbergs are still away," said the girl, whose name was Kat.

Thora absorbed the news with a frown. "When will they come back?"

"End of the month. It's their annual trip to Venice to see the new movies."

Suddenly Thora felt quite lonely. She wished she had

some friends. She wished that she didn't have to live on land.

When Kat saw her lip tremble, she held out a box of tissues. "Twenty cents each," she said. "You'll have the theater to yourself today. The rain has kept everyone away. Nobody will see you crying."

"I seem to cry at the flick of a tail these days," said Thora, helping herself. "Maybe it's all the rain we're getting. And then there's Cosmo. He looks so glum that he makes *me* want to cry. Together we really are a field and valley of tears." She paid and went in.

In some ways, it was an ordinary old-fashioned theater with rows of dusty plush velvet seats and heavy maroon curtains and steep aisles that felt sticky underfoot.

But Thora, who had never been inside such a cinema before, looked around her in wonder. The chandelier overhead reminded her of a great jeweled fish. The organ at the front resembled the pipe organ she'd glimpsed in a Greek Orthodox church in Thessalonika. She found a seat in the front row. As the lights dimmed and the screen filled with colored images, she felt something magical was about to happen.

For two full hours, Thora forgot about everything except the story unfolding before her. When the movie finished, she stood up and stretched and flopped back into her squeaky chair, hoping to make the feeling last. Eventually Kat shone her flashlight in Thora's face and asked her to leave.

"I could watch that again and again and again." Thora sighed.

"I do," said Kat. "Sometimes three times per day."

"You are so lucky to work in a cinema. They're very romantic places, aren't they? The movie was a bit sad, but that's what I liked about it." She clasped Kat's hand. "Maybe *I* might get a job here. What do you think? You wouldn't even have to pay me. I could sweep up candy wrappers and popcorn kernels—that sort of thing."

"We don't need any help," said Kat coldly.

"But we *all* need a little help," said Thora. "My mother always says, 'Don't kick a gift sea horse in the mouth.' I'm Thora, by the way."

Kat followed Thora to the door.

"I'll be back," said Thora. "Good-bye."

"Not so fast," said Kat. "What is *this*?" She shone the torch on Thora's feet. She then followed the wet trail back into the cinema to Thora's seat. "I don't believe it! You've spilled your drink everywhere!"

"Must be from the rain," sang Thora. "I didn't have a drink."

"I'll bet you don't do this at home."

"Well, now that you mention it . . ."

"*Just go*," said Kat, pushing the mop across the dollar-sized drips.

After Kat had put the mop away and locked the front doors and turned off the television set and the popcorn machine, she took out a new piece of white chalk.

Under the word *Banished* she added another name.

Thora.

CHAPTER
32

MEANWHILE, WORD HAD GOT AROUND GRIMLI that a strange girl was living alone on the *Loki* with her pet peacock. At the regular Monday town council meeting, parents and teachers stood up and declared that no child should be living without adult supervision. On Tuesday the Children's Aid Society was contacted. Foster parents were alerted. On Wednesday a photograph of Thora appeared in the *Daily Seasider* along with an urgent appeal:

ABANDONED CHILD NEEDS HOME!

Thora is approximately ten years old. She is energetic and resourceful, and at present does not seem to realize that she has been abandoned by a certain Mr. Walters. She appears to love animals and bright colors and possibly onion rings. If you can be a foster parent to this little girl, please contact Mrs. Honey Grubb at the Grimli Police Station.

Thora howled as she read the article to her mother and Cosmo. "Listen to this! They say I am *little*! Imagine!" She stood up to remind Halla and Cosmo that she was tall for her age. Cosmo nodded. "I suppose I do love bright colors. And animals. Certainly not Doberman pinchers or March flies or scorpions. And terns are a bit scary. Remember when we were in Bass Strait and the tern dive-bombed Mr. Walters and pecked his scalp?" She shivered and gave Cosmo a hug. "But *you're* all right. Now where are the scissors? This article belongs in my journal!"

Halla was silent as she watched her daughter rifle through the kitchen drawers looking for scissors and glue. Of course, nobody knew that Halla was taking care of her daughter. But she didn't like the idea of Mrs. Grubb looking for a foster family.

"Don't worry, Mom," said Thora, pasting the article in her book. "I'm not going to go off with any frosted family. I have a family already! Now off to the bakery for a treat!"

Thora and Cosmo were sprawled on the floor stuffing themselves with cream doughnuts and Halla was tidying the kitchen drawers when they heard the *clop-clop-clopping* of hooves on the dock.

Thora raced to the window. "Here's a sight for sore eyes!" she shouted. Cosmo coughed and scratched. "Do you think he's for real?" Thora asked.

"Be careful," whispered Halla, disappearing down through the pizza-shaped hole.

The policeman climbing down off his horse was a magnificent sight in his tight scarlet tunic with its shiny gold buttons and his breeches and his knee-high leather boots. He whistled as he made his way over to the *Loki*.

"I'm looking for a girl named Thora," he said through the door.

Thora swallowed and nodded and threw open the door

and pointed at herself. "Well, you found her," she said.

"I've been asked to pay you a little visit."

"Lucky me," enthused Thora. "A real, live Grenadier de St. Martin. *Do* come in." She ushered the big man into the *Loki* and offered him a seat on an old apple crate, then handed him a doughnut. "I haven't laid eyes on one of you since a member of your troop arrested my mother in Buenos Aires for taking a dip in a fish tank."

"Sorry to disappoint you," he said, "but I'm a police officer."

"No need to be sorry!" she said. "I'm not!"

It was then that she noticed that Cosmo had eaten the cream out of all the doughnuts. She was wondering what to do, as it seemed a bit mean to serve doughnuts without cream, when the crate on which the policeman was sitting collapsed under him.

"Oops-a-daisy!" he said, springing to his feet.

Thora scooped up the doughnut and rushed into the bathroom. She searched Mr. Walters's shaving kit. "Phew!" she said, flipping the cap off a tall green bottle marked "Brute Shaving Cream—For all skin types." She shook it and pressed the top and hey presto, a wonderful dollop of soft, white foam appeared. She was so pleased that she shook and squirted a few more times.

Then she ran back and handed the officer the doughnut.

He admired it and took a bite.

"Fresh from the bakery an hour ago," she said. She had never sampled shaving cream before. The smell was a little musky for her taste. "How is it?" she asked anxiously.

"Delicious!"

"There's more!" she cried, delighted. "Won't be a minute."

In the bathroom she squirted what was left of the shaving cream onto the remaining doughnuts. "Excuse my fingers," she said, handing one to the policeman.

"Never mind," he said, with his mouth full of doughnut. "Now, getting back to the reason I came. It seems that you are living here all by yourself. Correct?"

"Incorrect."

The policeman checked the notes on his clipboard. "Hmm," he said. "Do you mind if I sit over there?" He pointed to the big leather chair. He looked a little unwell.

"Please do," said Thora.

"Now," resumed the policeman. "It says here, quite clearly, that you are an orphan. And that I'm to help you gather your things together and then you are to come with me to headquarters, where we'll meet Mrs. Grubb, who will take you to meet the Rukles, your new foster family."

Thora sprang across the room and grabbed the policeman's hand. "I know a good game! It's called Statues!" She pulled him to his feet and spun him around.

"Now, now," he said. "Be a good girl and do as I say."

"No, you be a good policeman and do as *I* say. When I let go of your hand, you have to stand the way you land—frozen to the ground—and you're not allowed to move a muscle. That's why it's called Statues. Then when I press your button, you come to life. If you're a *good* statue, and by that I mean an *interesting* statue, the rich art expert might decide to purchase you for a museum. I play the art expert. Okay? Ready? Here we go!"

"I don't feel well," said the policeman, falling on all fours.

"Shhh!" She let her ponytail fall into her face. She scratched her elbows. She snapped her fingers. "Got it. You're a husky dog named . . . King, pulling an Inuit across the tundra. Mush! Mush!"

The policeman stood up. His tunic was streaked with shaving cream and his breeches were dusty from the floor. He headed for the door in fright.

"That's the broom cupboard!"

Too late. The broom and mop bumped him on the head.

"Don't you hate it when that happens!" sang Thora.

The policeman groaned.

"Let's get you some fresh air," said Thora. She guided him outside and, with an encouraging pat on the back, she helped him mount his horse. "Come back anytime. But be sure to call first. Then I can make sure that there are lots of cream doughnuts for you when you get here!"

"Oh, please, no!" he cried, and galloped off as fast as the horse's legs would carry him.

"Dogs don't talk!" she cried out after him.

Cosmo squawked.

"Yikes!" said Thora. "Some people don't understand the first thing about playing Statues!"

CHAPTER
33

"*FOOD POISONING?!*" SHRIEKED THE MAYOR'S WIFE.

"Food poisoning," said the chief of police.

"But he was sent there to collect the orphan, not to have a dinner party!"

"Alls I can tell you, Mrs. Grubb, is that he came back from the *Loki* green as a tree frog. Parked his tigers all over the front steps of the police station. Looked like cream doughnuts to me. I sent him home with orders to stay in bed until it passes."

"How you people can call yourselves professionals . . ."

"Sorry, ma'am. Want *me* to go and net her?"

"No. I'll do it myself."

That evening the chief of police delivered Thora a handwritten invitation from the mayor's wife:

Dear Thora,

I would be very charmed to meet you.

Would you like to come for lunch tomorrow?

We will eat egg salad sandwiches, tapioca pudding, and a beverage of your choice. We can discuss your future here in Grimli. I would like to help.

Drop by 12 Yegemewler Street at noon.

Yours sincerely,
Mrs. Honey Grubb

"Tickety-boo, Cosmo!" cried Thora. "Though mother won't be very happy about it." She slipped the invitation into her book. When Halla came by to say good night, Thora broke the news. "Our first lunch party on dry land!"

"I don't think you should go," said Halla, propping herself up on her elbows. "This woman wants to find you another family. You can write a letter of regret. I'll help you."

126

Thora shook her head. "I've already decided what I'm going to take her." From the freezer she produced an octopus-cheek casserole and, from the tea chest, a small figurine of Neptune that Halla had found on the bed of the great Icelandic salmon river, Langa. It was black and made of lava and thought to have been carved by one of the early Irish monks who sailed to Iceland in the fifth century.

"I don't want you to go," said Halla.

Thora put the statue in a small box, sprinkled some of Cosmo's angora neck fluff on it in case it got knocked about, and slipped it into the pocket of her Halla-Skin. "Mom, please stop worrying. I *want* to go. If I don't get out and about, how am I going to ever find my feet?"

That night Halla could not sleep. She sat on the Rock and stared in the direction of the *Loki* until the sky began to pale into morning. She felt sick with worry. What kind of a mother was she who could not protect her daughter from humans like Mrs. Grubb? The words *abandoned* and *foster family* rang hotly in her ears. Not for the first time, Halla wished that she had legs.

At noon the next day, Thora rang the bell of 12 Vegemewler Street. Mrs. Honey Grubb greeted her wearing a yellow pantsuit, rubber gloves, and a surgical mask. In one hand she carried a bottle of room spray. Her honey-colored hair was pulled back severely. She had small black eyes in a large flat face. She welcomed Thora in with a *Pssssss! Pssssss!* from her spray bottle.

"Did I interrupt something?" coughed Thora.

She bowed and held out her hand, but Mrs. Grubb did not take it. Instead, Mrs. Grubb removed her mask and let it dangle around her neck like a necklace.

"I was just doing a spot of dusting," she explained. "Do come in. How lovely to see you, Thora. And look! Don't tell me you've brought some food! You shouldn't have, really. You're going to show me up!"

Thora handed Mrs. Grubb the casserole and glanced around the living room. The furniture, including a piano, was covered with what looked like plastic wrap. The plants were fake, the carpet was streaked with vacuum stripes, and the lights were of a fluorescence so bright that they hurt Thora's eyes. The room reminded Thora of the quarantine station in London where they'd been forced to board Cosmo back when Halla swam the English Channel.

"Do excuse my gloves," said Mrs. Grubb, sniffing the casserole. "I have a *condition*. I wear them to protect my immune system."

"Oh, yes," enthused Thora. "I totally agree."

"With what?"

"It is *very important* to protect both the solar system *and* the moon system. I think the moon system must feel a little left out sometimes, what with the sun getting all the attention. Personally, I prefer the moon. It's prettier, and you can look at it without hurting your eyes."

Mrs. Grubb frowned. "My immune system was depleted last year because of all the charity work I do. My husband, the mayor, is always at me to slow down and put myself first. You see, I'm one of those people who sees a problem and just *has to help*. Some people are born that way, you know. The problem is, I've worn out my immune system, and now I am allergic to hair spray, nail polish remover, perfume, tomatoes, water, air, and *especially* to peacocks. I'm afraid you cannot bring that beast with you. You're going to have to get rid of it eventually. It's against the rules for foster children to bring their pets to their new house. But for now, tie it to the fence post. Here's a chain. I always keep several on hand. You never know when you might need one."

"Oh, that's not necessary," said Thora. "Cosmo will head on home by himself."

Thora waved at Cosmo and followed Mrs. Grubb into the dining room. The air was stuffy, and the room smelled like a freshly sanitized public toilet. Thora's eyes and nose began to water.

"I knew it," said Mrs. Grubb. "A sickly orphan girl."

"Where?" asked Thora, looking around.

Mrs. Grubb handed her a box of tissues. "Have a blow," she said. "I always keep them on hand just in case."

"Oh, that's okay. I usually just use my sleeve."

"Poor thing. You haven't been *socialized*, have you?"

"Well, I'm not sure. What's that?"

"Nobody has taken the time to teach you *manners*. To teach you how a young lady ought to behave." She opened a closet door and pulled out a shopping bag. "But all that is about to change." Her lips tightened. "Here's a little something to get you launched into your new life."

"A present? For me?" said Thora, touching the box in

her pocket containing the statue of Neptune. Somehow she didn't think Mrs. Grubb would like it. "That's very thoughtful!" said Thora. Mrs. Grubb passed her the bag, and Thora removed the bundle inside. It was wrapped in yellow tissue paper. Thora sneezed. "What is it?"

"A dress," said Mrs. Grubb.

"Thank you, but I don't really wear dresses," said Thora, recalling Halla's warning about hiding her scales.

"It's not just *any* dress," said Mrs. Grubb sharply. "It's a school uniform!"

"You're kidding!" Thora laughed, holding it up. "But I don't go to school."

"You will soon. Now try it on. There's a bathroom over there. Don't dawdle!"

In the bathroom, Thora pulled the dress on over her wetsuit. It was made from a light cotton material with a pattern of blue and white checks. It had a Peter Pan collar and buttons up the front.

"It's not very waterproof," said Thora as she emerged from the bathroom.

"Silly girl! First you'll have to remove that dreadful black suit you're wearing."

"My *Halla-Skin*? That's impossible!" said Thora.

"Don't be ridiculous. Take it off this instant, and then I'll take you over to the school and enroll you, and then we'll go and meet your foster family, the Rukles."

"No," said Thora slowly. "You see, I have a 'condition' myself."

Mrs. Grubb narrowed her eyes. "Is that right?"

"Yes, ma'am."

"Well, I can't say I'm surprised. All that sneezing! That running nose! What is it?"

"It's called Diam Rem."

"I don't think I've heard of that one. *Diam rem.* Hmm. Is that the Latin name? Let me get my *Big Book of Common Illnesses and Ailments.*"

"No!" cried Thora. "It won't be in there . . . it's not very *common.*"

"A rare condition. Is it contagious?"

"Only if I remove my Halla-Skin."

Mrs. Grubb frowned. "Is it fatal?"

"Not exactly. It's more of a . . . *choronic* sort of condition. I'll have it for the rest of my life. It's something I've had to learn to live with. I'm used to it now, but I need to spend a lot of time near water. Outside, you know. That's why school won't work out very well."

"All children must attend school. Especially orphans in need of socialization. Anyway, I've never heard of it." She sniffed. "*Diam rem.* Were you diagnosed by a proper doctor or a quack?"

Thora leaned forward and pulled up one of the legs of her wet suit to reveal a purple ankle. Under the fluorescent light, her scales came into sharp focus.

Mrs. Grubb gasped and reached for her face mask. "Let us be off!"

CHAPTER

34

FIRST MRS. GRUBB TOOK THORA TO the local primary school. Although the term did not begin for another month, she wanted Thora to meet the principal. "There's someone I want to introduce you to," she told her.

The school was a long, low building the color of pale sand, and on the main door, a sign read:

"Oh, dear," said Thora. "We didn't bring flowers!"

"Flowers?"

Thora pointed to the sign. "When Mr. Walters had his hip replacement operation, I used to visit him at the hostable in Salisbury, and these signs were everywhere."

"This is not a hospital. It's a school."

"A school?" said Thora. "But I thought schools were made out of redbrick and had a bell at the entrance and a fire escape out the side. At least that's what the school looks like in *Tom Brown's School Days*."

They entered and made their way down a long empty corridor with gleaming linoleum floors that creaked underfoot. "It certainly smells like a hostable. Well, actually, it smells a little like your house, Mrs. Grubb."

"That's the disinfectant," said Mrs. Grubb. "Not something I'd expect that you've come across very much in your life."

In a small office stacked with papers, books, and brown cardboard boxes, Mrs. Grubb folded away her face mask and pressed a buzzer. "He said he'd meet us in here. Now where is he?"

Thora ran over and picked a book up off a trolley. "*Harry Potter and the Sorcerer's Stone*. I wonder if this book is about Mr. Walters's artist friend, the hairy potter from Cape Town."

"I doubt it," said Mrs. Grubb.

"He had the bushiest blackest moustache I've ever seen. And a beard and a ponytail down to his waist that he fastened with a twist-tie! He even had tufts of hair sprouting out of his ears and from the tops of his fingers! Oh, and before I forget, he also had hair on his chest and his back. He said it was terribly hot in the summer, like wearing a black sheepskin vest around, and that he'd thought about having it all removed, zapped with a laser, like an Olympic swimmer does."

"My goodness, you do chatter on."

"Interestingly, he didn't have any hair on the top of his head. His hairline started just above his ears." She fluffed out her ponytail. "Mr. Walters said that hair patterns are inherited through the mother's line. So the potter must have had a very interesting-looking mother!"

"I can't abide hairy men. He sounds horrid."

"Oh, no, he was a sparky person and very good at his trade. He let me have a go on his potter's wheel, but I'm afraid my pot caved in. Potting requires a delicate touch. Have you ever thrown a pot, Mrs. Grubb?"

"I may take it up if you don't shut up. You're making my sinuses ache. Oh, now, here he comes. Hello, Mr. Mason!"

"I'm sorry to keep you waiting."

"Think nothing of it. We were just admiring all your excellent books, weren't we, Thora?"

"I'd love to read this book about Mr. Walters's friend, the hairy potter from Cape Town."

Mr. Mason gave a puzzled smile. "A fine book! And a favorite with many children. It's great to see them reading. As a principal you can't ask for much more, can you? Heh heh heh. You may borrow it if you like."

"Thanks," sang Thora, tucking it into the pocket in her wet suit, next to the little statue of Neptune.

"Now," said Mrs. Grubb. "We were hoping to register Thora so she can start school next term."

Mr. Mason pulled out a pile of papers from a drawer of his desk. "Okay, let's get the ball in motion here. Let me see. What grade have you completed to date, Thora?"

"I'm afraid I don't understand the question."

"How far have you progressed with your formal education?"

"I've never gone to school. So I reckon not very far, formally."

"Never?"

"Nope."

"And why is that, Thora?"

"These sound like trick questions to me." Thora frowned, scratching her elbows. "I guess it's because I've been very busy."

"Busy doing what?"

"'Living between worlds' is how my mother puts it."

"Stop talking rubbish," said Mrs. Grubb impatiently.

"Mr. Walters has said that I'll probably have to attend school eventually, but that the first four years are a complete waste of time anyway. He's always said I have learned much more from reading books and traveling than I ever would from sitting in alphabetical order in a moldy old classroom."

Mr. Mason laced his fingers together and put his hands on his chest. "Is Mr. Walters a qualified teacher?"

"Oh, no. He would never become a teacher. He is a *man of the world*."

"But you can read, I presume?"

"Oh, yes. Mr. Walters taught me when I was four."

"What sort of books?"

"Oh, you know, whatever Mr. Walters managed to have airlifted to the *Loki*."

"Such as?"

"Let's see. *The Annotated Biography of Donald Bradman*, the cricketer, was a good one. I also enjoyed *Njal's Saga*."

"Njal's what?"

"Saga. It's set in medieval Iceland—a ripping tale! The chieftain, Njal, was beardless—not like the hairy potter from Cape Town! Author unknown. It's quite an olden-time story, though not as olden-time as the Bible, I don't think. What else? Let me see. . . ."

Mr. Mason changed tack. "Travel and reading are fine and good," he said. "But school teaches you things like mathematics."

"What, like quadratic equations and calculus?"

"Well, we start with arithmetic and move on to those when you are older."

"What's the point of going backward? It would be a shame to unlearn what I know already. And a lot of work to learn it again!"

Mr. Mason tried another new slant. "In the classroom, you will learn discipline."

"My mother taught me that when she swam the lakes and rivers of the world."

"And manners."

Thora bowed, a three-quarter bow that she had been taught in Tokyo. "Did you know that in Japan it is considered rude to smile at a stranger?" She paused. "One thing that does interest me about school . . ."

"Yes?" said Mr. Mason.

"It's something I read about in *Anne of Green Gables*. Does each student really get a *slate* to write on? Do you remember the way she hit Gilbert Blythe over the head with her slate because he called her 'carrots'? I'd do the same, I think, though I would have forgiven him faster than Anne. She was a proud old thing. But you often see that in red-haired people—have you noticed?"

"We've moved on from then," said Mr. Mason. "Our students use pens and paper."

"Fountain pens with silver nibs that you dip in black inkwells? Mr. Walters uses Sir Josiah Mason 1002 fine point. They're quite hard to get hold of. He's only been able to find them at the Royal College of Art in London. He calls it the Great World Nib Shortage."

"*Ballpoint* pens."

"That's too bad," said Thora. "They blot when you carry them in your pocket."

"I think school will do this girl a world of good," said Mr. Mason to Mrs. Grubb. "She'll learn to be quiet and respectful. And she'll study proper subjects like social studies and science."

"It's so strange when people talk about you as if you're not there!" observed Thora. "But perhaps that is one of the customs around here. One never knows exactly how to judge these matters. Each country is so different."

"What is your surname, Thora?"

"Surname? I don't think I have one."

"That's nonsense. Everyone has a last name. What was your father's surname?"

"My father died before I was even born," Thora said slowly. "And my mother never found it out, because it wasn't part of her culture to have a family name. What about a surname from *Njal's Saga*? Those characters had rather interesting last names. You can call me Thora Mord Fiddle if you like."

Mr. Mason sighed. "That will do for now, Thora. You will start in Mr. Butterfield's class in one month's time. On your first day of class, please report to room four wearing the regulation blue-and-white-checked uniform that I understand Mrs. Grubb has generously purchased for you with her own money. I would also like you to wear proper shoes on your feet."

"I'm sorry, that's out of the question."

"Why is that?"

"My second toe is much longer than my big toe. Regular shoes don't fit."

Mr. Mason looked down at Thora's feet. "We don't let our students wear wind-surfing slippers to class."

Mrs. Grubb whispered something into Mr. Mason's ear.

"*Diam rem*?" said Mr. Mason. "Never heard of it. I'd like her to have a proper medical checkup, too."

Thora shrugged. "Not all doctors are familiar with the condition."

Mr. Mason sighed. "I think we'll skip the tour of the school, Mrs. Grubb. Good day."

CHAPTER
35

THE TOWN WAS SMALL, AND SO they didn't have to walk far before they came to the Rukle residence, a house badly in need of a paint job. There was a swing set and a sandbox and a red plastic schoolhouse and, off to one side, a badminton net. Thora's foster parents were waiting behind a gate with a sign attached to it:

In a flash, Thora realized she'd seen them before.

The pale, red-eyed Mrs. Rukle was the woman she'd seen sobbing on the beach on the night of the storm.

And the fat man was the bully who'd grabbed Ricky by the scruff of the neck on the pier—she'd seen him at the Tooty Frooty, too, playing the slot machines.

As she followed the couple up the walkway, the tough little dog that Ricky had called Tiny Stevens began to bark. The door slammed, and two children emerged from the house.

Ricky laughed when he saw Thora. "You!" he said, looking down at Thora's feet.

"Thora, meet your new brother and sister," said Mrs. Grubb. "Ricky and Lynne. Now you children run off and play while I finalize some of the paperwork."

The children were grateful to be released.

"I can't believe it's *you*!" said Ricky. "I never told them, just like you asked. The coast guard said I was really lucky. They'd never seen the wind die down so suddenly. It was practically *supernatural*."

"Are you a witch?" asked Lynne, chewing at a fingernail. She had pale blonde hair cut in a straight fringe above her glasses, and her feet were bare. "Can I see your feet?"

"Maybe later," said Thora. "Now what do we have here?"

They showed Thora their toys. The swing was too small for Thora. The badminton rackets were coming unstrung. And the posts holding up the badminton net were rotten and fell over when Thora tapped them. Although it all looked cheerful from a distance, the sad truth was that everything was falling apart. Even the little schoolhouse was blackened on one side where someone had tried to set it on fire.

"We set this all up this morning for you," said Ricky. "Normally Dad says toys are for spoiled brats."

"We found it all at the garbage dump," said Lynne.

The children explained to Thora that they were very poor. Mr. Rukle had lost all his money at the Tooty Frooty. He was addicted to the slot machines. "Mother feels tired all the time and has to have long rests on the couch. Mr. and Mrs. Grubb are going to give us money to have you."

"That's nice. How much?" asked Thora.

"Enough to make it worthwhile," said Lynne.

Thora picked up the schoolhouse and held it over her head. "Let's take this garbage back to where it belongs."

Ricky and Lynne smiled. "We don't like them anyway."

"They don't even work."

"They're no fun."

"Of course not," said Thora. "You know why?"

"Why?"

"Because they were made by extremely stupid grown-ups. Now if it were up to children, there wouldn't be these sorts of toys. No more plastic teacups and itty-bitty doll houses (although I don't mind the occasional plastic peacock, I must say). No more Junior Scrabble and miniature badminton sets that break after the first game and furry little animals made out of nylon. Why, when there are proper hammers, and games with rules that make sense, and real live cuddly furry warm animals that can sleep on your bed with you at night?"

She threw the schoolhouse up into the air and Ricky caught it.

"Why have a plastic school when you live down the street from a real one?" She pointed and broke into a trot. "C'mon!"

The children followed Thora into the school playground. Thora opened an unlocked window and they sneaked inside.

"This is the best way to go to school," said Thora. "When you're not supposed to!"

The room they found themselves in was quiet. The smell of chalk and gym shoes hung in the air. They examined the large map of the world on the wall. Thora rifled through the teacher's desk and found some bright yellow highlighters. "Let's each mark where in the world we've been."

Ricky and Lynne found the area where Grimli was, and Thora colored it yellow.

"Now, where else?"

Ricky and Lynne looked at each other. "Our grandmother is from England," said Lynne.

"But we've never been there," said Ricky. "Or anywhere else."

Thora looked at them in astonishment. "How terrible!" she said. "Then why not color in all the places you'd *like* to go?"

"I'd like to go to the circus," said Lynne.

"Okay," said Thora, coloring in Russia. "There is an excellent circus in Moscow, which has people who can tie themselves in knots and men who can be shot out of a cannon through rings of fire into the jaws of hippopotamuses."

Lynne smiled. "Oh, yes, let's go to Russia! Like Eloise in *Eloise in Moscow*."

"Yes," said Thora. "She had a good life full of travel and adventure—though she didn't get to see much of her mother."

"That would be horrible," said Lynne.

"It depends, I guess," said Thora thoughtfully.

It was Ricky's turn. He looked dreamily out of the window. "I want to go to the Rock," he said.

"That's *so boring*," said Lynne. "Thora means a real place. Out in the world."

"The Rock *is* a real place," said Ricky.

"Okay," said Thora, "but it's not marked on the map. Where else do you want to go?"

He thought for a while. "Someplace to swim with dolphins."

"Righty-o," said Thora. "We've got a few options for that. How about Zanzibar? After the dolphins, you can have a fruit fight with a monkey. *Jambo, jambo*! And chase potbellied pigs and eat chicken satay with peanut butter sauce! Yum!"

They heard a crackle and, from a speaker over the clock, a voice. "Who's there?"

"Time to split," whispered Thora. "Shhh."

Lynne began to chew her fingernails. "That's the principal, Mr. Mason. He'll beat us with the board of education."

"I'll tan his hide if he tries such a thing," said Thora indignantly.

Their voices were drowned out by the sound of a burglar alarm.

They slipped back out through the window and into the playground. They ran as fast as they could to the fence. Thora helped the other two over and tossed them the toy schoolhouse, then climbed over herself.

"Stop running," said Thora. "Walk! Be casual."

Just then a police car turned onto the street. It was heading for the school! Thora waved.

"What are you doing?" whispered Ricky, frightened.

The car slowed and the policeman peered out at them. "You know anything about this business with the school?" he asked suspiciously.

"Absolutely." Thora nodded. "Someone's tried to set it on fire. Luckily, the damage is minimal. In fact, one hardly notices it. I say, officer, why don't you ride a horse like your good colleague?"

The policeman frowned, ignoring her last remark. "Fire?"

"Yes," she said, pointing out the burned side of the plastic schoolhouse. "Could you suggest where we should take it for repairs? Actually," she added, "we've outgrown it, as children do—but some little child might find it amusing."

"I've got a little boy, two years old, who would like it," said the policeman. He looked over to the real building, relieved that she was only talking about a toy. "I'll buy it from you. For five dollars."

Thora let her hair fall into her face. "Fifteen," she said. "Not including delivery."

They settled on ten. Thora gave five to Ricky and five to Lynne.

"Put it in the trunk and I'll drive you home."

"Oh, yes!" cried Ricky. "A ride in a real live cop car!"

The policeman let them look at his radio and touch some of the important-looking buttons. He even took them on a little detour through town. As he drove, he told them that he had always wanted to be a policeman.

"It's nice when dreams come true!" sang Thora.

Finally his radio beeped and a crackly voice said, "Where the dickens are you? We've had a B&E over at the school. Over."

"What's that?" said Thora.

"Break and enter," said the policeman. He dropped them home and sped off, siren blaring.

CHAPTER
36

MR. RUKLE WAS WAITING ON THE steps. He had removed his jacket and wore a grimy T-shirt with big sweat stains under the armpits. His face was purple. Big veins pulsed on his temple like a frog's heartbeat. "What have you been up to now?" he said. "No lies."

"We've been having a wonderful time," said Thora.

"With that cop? What sort of trouble are you in? Get inside, the three of you."

The children darted into the house and through to the kitchen, where Ricky and Lynne stood staring at the floor.

Thora did a cartwheel. *Smuch!* went her wind-surfing slippers. "We were only away for half an hour," she said, checking her watch. "Then the policeman gave us a ride home. He was a nice chap, wasn't he, Lynne? Hey, where's Mrs. Grubb?"

"Clam it. She got fed up waiting for you." He pointed his sausage finger so close to Thora's face that she had to cross her eyes to follow it. "She needs you to sign some form before she can give us the money. She had to rush off to get to some fancy dinner at the Tooty Frooty. So we still haven't been paid."

He swung around to glare at Lynne and Ricky. "Whaddya staring at? Hey! What's that?" He tore the five-dollar bill out of Lynne's hand. "Did you steal it? I should have guessed. Go to the Punishment Room. And you, Ricky, go and chop some wood." He cuffed him on the ear.

"Ouch!" shouted Ricky.

"Shut your trap! Your mother has a headache. Time to start thinking about other people for once in your lives." He turned to Thora. "And you!" he shouted, nose hairs dancing. "I think we need to get a few things straight around here."

"Yes, we do," said Thora, fascinated. "Such as, why are you performing the *haka* without a grass skirt?"

From the stairs, Lynne gasped.

Mr. Rukle spluttered.

"I thought all Maori dancers wore grass skirts. I may not be remembering correctly, though, as I was only very tiny when my mother swam the Great Bear River near Wellington."

"Button your lip, missy, or I'll do it for you!"

Thora laughed heartily. "Good one! *Button your lip.* That's one of the things I just *love* about living in a new place. All the unique vertinacular expressions you come across. I wonder if that phrase translates well into Russian. Lynne will find out when she goes to see the circus in Moscow!"

Lynne rushed up the stairs into the Punishment Room.

"Get over here, girl," said Mr. Rukle, rolling up his sleeves. "It's time to teach you a lesson."

"Oh, no, thanks. I'd rather do the *haka.* The All Blacks

do it before their football games." She leaned forward and made her eyes pop and stuck out her tongue in the style of Maori dancers.

Mrs. Rukle peeked into the kitchen. Mr. Rukle's back was turned, so he didn't see her, and that was lucky, because she was smiling. She looked quite pretty. Then she disappeared again.

"*Do the haka!*" shouted Thora.

Mr. Rukle stamped his feet and waved his arms and the purple veins on his temples wiggled and danced. The five dollars he had taken from Lynne sailed to the floor.

"That's the way!" cheered Thora, scooping up the bill.

He grabbed her ponytail, but she yanked it out of his hand, limbo danced under his arm, and scampered up onto the kitchen table.

"I'm gonna get you!" he cried furiously.

Thora threw open the window and slipped out into the backyard. "Pssss!" she said, looking up at the window on the second floor. "Lynne!" Lynne opened the window. Thora removed the box containing the little lava statue of Neptune from her pocket, wrapped it in the five-dollar bill, and tossed it up into Lynne's outstretched hand.

"It won't pay for your journey to Moscow, but every little bit helps!"

"Bye, Thora!"

"Cheerio!" Thora waved. "Send me a postcard from the circus!"

Back at the *Loki*, Cosmo greeted Thora with a fan of the tail. He led her immediately to the hole and indicated for her to turn on the light.

Halla was swimming in frantic circles below the boat. When she saw the light, she shot up through the hole. "You're home!" she cried, gathering Thora into a shimmery hug. "I've been so worried! Tell me everything!"

"The worst part of it," said Thora as she came to the end of her story, "was the dress. I feel *so sorry* for human girls who have to wear those horrid things!"

CHAPTER
37

TWO WEEKS LATER, ON A LAZY Thursday afternoon, as Thora was painting a picture of a sea dragon on her bedroom wall and pondering whether sea dragons had belly buttons, she heard the *bzzz* and *whirlll* of Frooty de Mare's plane landing once again in the harbor.

"The de Mares are back, Cosmo," she said, rinsing her paintbrush in a cup of cold tea.

A polite knock came on the door.

"Hello there! Come on in!"

Holly handed her a glossy flyer. "I can't stay. I'm delivering promotional material for my father's business."

Thora looked down at the sheet.

FROOTY DE MARE
WOULD LIKE TO ANNOUNCE
THE OPENING OF HIS

NEW CINEMA!

COME AND CELEBRATE WITH US on FRIDAY NIGHT!
FREE onion rings and popcorn balls!
Balloons for the kids!
POP!
FUN FOR all!

"New cinema?" said Thora. "Grimli already *has* a cinema."

"I know," said Holly. "But the Allbent Cinema is very out-of-date. My dad's cinema will be much nicer. And he'll show better, more up-to-date films."

Thora considered this. "The more the merrier!" she said. "I'll be there! But it's tomorrow night. Could I have a few extra flyers? I'd like to give one to the Rukles."

Holly looked surprised. "You know the Rukles?"

"Yep. I almost moved in with them."

"They used to be my best friends," said Holly.

"Used to be? How sad," said Thora.

"My father says they're rough and common and that they're going nowhere fast." She remembered how Lynne had told her that Mr. Rukle had lost all his money on the slot machines.

"Oh, no," said Thora. "They've got big plans. In fact, Lynne is going to Moscow and Ricky is considering Zanzibar."

Once again she invited Holly in. "You still haven't heard our singing kettle!"

This time Holly relented.

"Did you realize," said Thora, setting out their best china teacups on the kitchen table, "that we don't even know each other's *names*? I'm Thora."

"Holly de Mare."

Thora's eyes widened. "Well, why didn't you say so before? What a beautiful name! *Holly*. My mother used to wear a wreath of holly around her neck as a necklace. Only at Christmastime, of course."

Holly smiled and revealed two dimples in each cheek.

"The fact is, holly berries are extremely poisonous."

The dimples vanished. "No, they're not."

"Yes, they are. I knew a girl who thought they were so beautiful that she ate an entire bowl of them. With cream and sugar. God rest her soul."

"She died?"

"Dead as a doornail. She didn't even have the fortitude to write out a will."

"Her poor parents!"

Thora tapped Holly's shoulder. "See what my ma bequeathed to me?" She twirled, and the medals around her waist clanged together.

"Your mother has . . . passed away?"

"'Course not," said Thora.

"Then where is she?" asked Holly, looking around for signs of a mother.

"It's a long story," said Thora. "Let's just say she's away

157

for a while . . . swimming."

"Swimming? Why?"

"Why not?"

"Where?"

"Where do you think!" exclaimed Thora, pointing to the water all around them.

Holly started to look worried. "I have to go. I'll get in trouble if these aren't delivered."

"It's up to you," said Thora, popping a cod cheek into her mouth. The kettle began to sing, and Thora joined in. "'Oh Susannah, oh won't you come with me . . .'"

Holly hesitated. She had never met a girl like Thora before. "Did the holly-berry girl have a funeral or anything?"

"Well, now the story gets interesting. They wanted to bury her, of course."

Holly nodded.

"But the earth was too frozen to manage this. Permafrost, you see. Ten feet down. Digging was out of the question. And so they placed the girl on an iceberg and let her float away to heaven."

"Terrible!"

"Oh, not at all. It was very romantic. They gave her a terrific send-off. Everyone in town came. They covered her with a caribou skin and a Hudson Bay blanket. Then they protected her spirit with a little fence of whale teeth. She was really very comfortable. But the best part is this: As she floated away, a baby seal jumped up on her iceberg and tickled her with his whiskers. And the girl woke up!"

Holly brightened. "She didn't die?"

"Not in the end, thanks to the seal. Seals are a lot of fun. They swim upside down."

"They do?"

"Yes, siree!"

"Why?"

"Why? Because it's *fun*! Why don't you give it a whirl?"

Holly folded her arms across her chest. "You're making this whole story up. I don't believe you. Not a word!"

"Well . . . she *did* get sick on the berries." Thora shrugged.

Holly's cheeks reddened. "It's wicked to tell lies."

"I've said nothing that didn't almost sort of happen."

"You've made everything up."

"Well, *my mother* likes my stories. They kept her awake as she swam the lakes and rivers of the world. Anyway, let me ask you something. Do you want to come to the cinema with me tonight?"

"Oh, yes!" answered Holly immediately. Then her face fell. "But I can't. Not to the Allbent. And anyway, my father's cinema opens tomorrow night. Then I can go to as many films as I like."

"Why can't you go to the Allbent?"

"It's a family rule. My dad is feuding with the Greenberg sisters."

"Rules are made to be broken," said Thora. "Or at least bent. No harm in asking. Let's go beg."

CHAPTER
38

THORA WANTED TO MAKE A GOOD impression on Holly's parents, and so she asked Holly to wait a moment.

She went off to her room and hauled out the tea chest from under the bed to hunt for a gift for the de Mares. A snorkel? A fish bone? A gold medal? Hmm. Then she saw the old set of teeth. "They're a little dirty," she said, sashaying into the main room. "But what do you expect from a scurvy pirate?"

She linked arms with Holly and they set off.

"I'm not sure this is a good idea," said Holly.

"Scared, are you?" Thora held Holly's hand. "I was scared once too." She paused. "Well, maybe other times. But I remember this one in particularity."

"When?"

"Oh, just last year, after my mother swam the Strait of Juan de Fuca. I went for a long walk on the beach, and the sun went down. I had to turn back in the dark. It was completely black. No moon. Suddenly the beach began to rustle. I took a step, and something crackled under my foot and squeezed up through my toes. And I had to walk at least a mile back down the beach."

"What was it that crackled?"

"Sea crabs. They come out each night and cover the beach. I would have just swum back, but I figured it was better to step on them than swim through them."

Holly shivered.

"Aw, they were harmless. I do feel bad now about the ones I squashed, though."

They paused for a moment outside the de Mares' cabin cruiser.

"Don't be scared," said Thora.

CHAPTER
39

THE LIVING ROOM OF THE CABIN cruiser resembled the lobby of the Tooty Frooty. The walls were gold, and the carpet was purple. The three de Mare brothers lay on the floor before a huge television screen.

"It smells like sea cow in here!" said Thora.

Holly pointed to a mountain of sneakers and held her nose.

Thora nodded. "Do they ever wash?"

"Never," said Holly.

"Do they speak?"

"Not much," said Holly.

"Why the red polka dots on their faces?"

"Shh!" said Holly. Then she whispered into Thora's ear. "They're pimples! Mother says that they get them from my father's family. They stand in the mirror and squeeze them. I've seen them pop!"

Mermaids did not get pimples. Thora was intrigued.

"Excuse me," she said, poking one of the brothers. "Is it true that if you squeeze a pinkle, it will pop?"

Three heads turned.

"Oh, look! You've *all* got pinkles! It's very festive! Why do you want to pop them?"

They grunted and turned back to watch the television.

Thora walked over and turned it off. "Televisions have the ability to hypnotize even the nicest people!"

The brothers stared at Thora. Nobody had ever *dared* to interrupt Saturday boxing. Not even their father would chance it!

"You're just like all the zombies playing the slot machines down at the Tooty Frooty!" she remarked, conversationally.

The biggest brother beat his chest and farted. The other two belched.

Then all at once, the three of them rose to their feet and surrounded her.

Darting out of their way, Thora pulled a gold medal from the chain around her waist and held it up. "*You are getting very sleepy,*" she said.

She had never tried to hypnotize anyone before. But she had seen Boris the Remarkable at the Monterey Bay Sea Show, and now she copied his technique. "I want you all to look at this medal. You are beginning to feel very sleepy. Your eyes are heavy."

She spoke in a low, soothing voice and let the medal swing back and forth.

Six small brown eyes followed it.

Six eyes began to droop.

Six eyes closed.

"Now when I clap my hands, you will all think you are . . . apes. Gorillas, to be more exact. Shy, sociable creatures. *Very* clean!"

She clapped her hands.

The boys began to grunt in a nice way. Then they smoothed the pillows on the sofa, seated themselves in a neat row, and began to check each other's heads for nits.

"Gorillas?" said Holly, her eyes wide.

"Gorillas are actually very nice primates," said Thora. "Grooming is their favorite activity—they can do it *all day long*!" She saw a comb resting on a table and she passed it to them.

Holly giggled. "Mom's been trying to get them to do

that for their whole lives!" She rushed out and returned with a bottle of perfume and some lipstick. "This will keep them busy for a while!"

The boys removed the atomizer from the bottle and took turns dousing each other. The air filled with the smell of wild magnolias. Thora sneezed. "My word!" she said. "It reminds me of the open swimming awards ceremony at the Four Seasons Hotel in Tripoli! Mother and I were rushed to the hospital with perfume poisoning!"

Mrs. de Mare bustled into the room. "It's very strange," she said, snapping on an earring, "but my favorite perfume has disappeared! The very expensive bottle that Daddy bought me in Paris."

A funny look came over her face.

"I'm afraid it's the lunkheads," said Thora.

Mrs. de Mare marched over. The perfume bottle lay on the floor, empty. They had moved on to the lipstick. One son was applying it in thick, red strips to another's lips. They reeked of wild magnolias.

Mrs. de Mare gasped and fell backward in a dead faint.

At that moment, the high whine of a speedboat could be heard outside. A few seconds later, the clatter of footsteps.

"Ooh!" said Holly.

The door burst open and her father staggered in.

Holly shrieked.

He was wearing his leather coat, but it was torn and wet and dripping with seaweed.

His face was puffed and bloody and one eye had swollen shut.

He was extremely happy.

He pointed to his wife, lying on the floor. "What's the matter with her?"

"She fainted!" sang Thora.

Mrs. de Mare began to groan. "Where am I?" She opened her eyes and gazed up at her husband.

"You're right here, Pussy-chops," he said. "Everything's all right." He smiled broadly.

Mrs. de Mare sat bolt upright. "Where are your two front teeth?"

Frooty had already been a little scary looking. But toothless, with one black eye and a bloodied face, he looked positively gruesome. He attempted to help his wife to her feet, but she smacked him away.

"What's happened?" asked Holly timidly.

"A miracle!" said Frooty. "The answer to all our dreams. The reward of all my labors. A miraculous, marvelous, and magical thing has happened." He gazed up at the ceiling, hugging himself in delight. "The opening of the cinema tomorrow is going to be fantastic!"

Everyone waited for him to finish. Even the boys looked over.

"But I can't tell you about it, tweety birds. Not yet."

"Well, how miraculous can it be if it's knocked out your two front teeth? Go look at yourself!" said Mrs. de Mare, furious. "How can we go out for dinner with you looking like a—"

"Pirate?" finished Thora helpfully. With a flourish, she held up the gift she had brought. "Here are some real pirate teeth."

CHAPTER

40

"WHO IS THIS . . . *CREATURE*?" ASKED MRS. DE MARE, aghast.

"The name is Thora."

Frooty was lost in his own world. He inspected himself in the mirror. "Hmm. Not good." He turned around. "Did you say *teeth*?"

"Pirate teeth," said Thora. "My mother found them off the coast of the Philippines, near Myanmar. The great-granddaughter of King Thibaw assured us that they were the real thing."

Frooty held them up to the light. "Whalebone?" he asked, impressed.

"Yep!" said Thora. "Try them on!"

"No," said Mrs. de Mare firmly. "He will go to a proper dentist."

"I will do no such thing," said Frooty.

"Daddy hates dentists," explained Holly.

"Take a seat and say 'ahhhh,'" said Thora.

"Ahhhh . . ."

"They fit!" she announced. "Just like Cinderella's slipper!" Then she pulled out the little cloth that she used to collect her mermaid drips and wiped Frooty's coat. "All you need now is an eye patch and Bob's your uncle!"

Frooty frowned. Holly had never brought home a friend like Thora. She was a strange girl. And oddly dressed. There was something, well . . . *fishy* about her.

"Hey!" he suddenly exclaimed, snapping his fingers. "Haven't I met you before?"

"Yep."

"You're the girl who said rude things about my stuffed mermaid!"

"That would be me," said Thora.

"Well, have I got a surprise for you!" said Frooty, laughing softly. "Now how much do I owe you for the teeth?"

"Parts and labor are free," replied Thora. "But there is one small favor I would like to ask."

"Ask away."

"It won't cost much."

"Then I'm sure it can be arranged."

"Two tickets to the Allbent tonight. For Holly and me."

The room fell silent. "No," he said. "You can go to my cinema when it opens tomorrow night."

"But you just said . . ." Holly plunged her face into her hands.

"The answer is *no*, you silly girl!" He pulled out a fifty-dollar bill. "Here. Take this. Go and buy yourselves a pizza or something. Rent a video. Have a nice time."

"What a wonderful idea!" said Mrs. de Mare brightly. "Aren't you lucky girls? You'll have a lovely time, I'm sure. And anyway, I don't know why you want to go to that revolting place when we have a perfectly good television set *right here.*"

CHAPTER
41

THE TWO GIRLS WAVED GOOD-BYE AND set off. It was a cool evening, with the smell of burning leaves in the air.

"I'm sorry I can't go to the Allbent," said Holly.

"Oh, you'll get there one day, I'm sure. I can feel it in my scales."

"Your scales?"

"Why doesn't your father like the sisters, anyway?" Thora asked quickly, changing the subject.

"Because they won't sell him the cinema. It sits on prime real estate, you know."

"It's a beautiful old building," said Thora.

"Oh, Daddy doesn't care about *that*. He'd tear it down and build a new one."

They walked for a few minutes in silence.

"There's nothing to do here." Holly sighed. "If we were in the city, we could go to the wave pool or the shopping mall. This town is *so* boring."

"Boring? This place?" To brighten Holly's mood, Thora did a cartwheel. "Ever tried to watch seaweed grow? Or take a time-lapse photo of a melting Finnish iceberg?"

Holly shook her head.

"That's *very* boring." She scratched her elbow. "I have an idea. Let's have a birthday party!"

"For who?

"For us."

"It's not my birthday. Is it yours?"

"Nope. But it was—and it will be again."

Holly gave this idea some thought. "We could dress up."

"And bake a birthday cake!"

"And sprinkle it with hundreds and thousands."

"Hundreds and thousands of what?"

Holly laughed. "Hundreds and thousands of *hundreds and thousands!*"

They paused in front of the all-night supermarket, the Tombody. "Maybe we should buy our birthday supplies in here," said Holly, dragging Thora in by the hand.

The supermarket was almost empty, but the aisles were well lit and full of foods that seemed strange to Thora. She rushed over to a section marked Frozen Foods. "Look," she said, perplexed, holding up a packet.

"Fish fingers," said Holly. "Mother used to cook those for us every night."

"But fish don't have *fingers*," said Thora. "And if they did, I certainly wouldn't want to eat them! And look over there. Rock cakes. Yuk!"

"Oh, no. Rock cakes are delicious," said Holly.

"Thora!" came a voice.

Thora turned to see Ricky and Lynne running down the aisle toward them.

"What are you doing here?" asked Ricky.

"Getting supplies for our birthday party. Wanna come?"

"Oh, yes! Whose birthday is it?"

"Everybody's!"

Mrs. Rukle appeared pushing a loaded shopping cart. She no longer looked pale and tired. In fact, she looked very well. Her cheeks were tinged with pink, and she had a nice new hairstyle.

"Hello, Thora," she said. "How are you?"

"All the better for seeing you!"

Ricky and Lynne asked their mother if they could join Thora's birthday celebration. She nodded. "I'll pick you up in a couple of hours."

"The more the merrier," said Thora.

Ricky and Lynne were very excited and couldn't wait to tell Thora their wonderful news. Their mother had used the ten dollars from the policeman to pay for an appraisal of the statue of Neptune that Thora had given them.

"*That* funny old thing!" said Thora. "I hope you scraped the lichen off it first!"

They had then sold the object to a dealer at Sotheby's in London for a lot of money—enough to leave Mr. Rukle and move into a new house on the other side of town!

And to pay for a brand-new secondhand car!

"Hurrah!" cried Thora.

When they found themselves in the Fresh Fruit and Vegetables section, Thora looked around. "Hey, where's Holly?"

"Holly?"

"She was with me a minute ago."

"Not Holly *de Mare!*" said Lynne.

"You mean Holly *de Nightmare!*" said Ricky.

"How odd," said Thora.

"She *is* odd."

"Don't you like her?" asked Thora, puzzled.

"We *used* to like her," said Ricky.

"Good! Then it will take no time at all for you to like her again."

They retraced their steps and found Holly crouching in the International Foods aisle under a sign advertising instant cappuccino.

"I found some of your old friends," said Thora. "Isn't it a small world! Like a connect-the-dots puzzle."

Holly took a deep breath. Then she whispered in Thora's ear, "They don't like me. They think I'm stuck-up."

"Stuck-up?" asked Thora. "Stuck up *what*?"

Lynne and Ricky folded their arms on their chests and looked away.

"Nobody is stuck up *anything,* as far as I can see," said Thora cheerfully. "Except that lady on the ladder. Hey, ma'am, is this where I'll find a tub of gentlemen's relish?"

The woman shook her head. "Never heard of it."

"What about gefilte fish?"

"Gefilte what?"

"Skyr?"

"Are you kidding?"

"Jeepers," whispered Thora. "They're not very well stocked. Let's go back to the *Loki*. The larder there is full. I'll make an angel food cake, and we'll get the party started."

CHAPTER
42

IT WAS AN ALTOGETHER BLEAK NOVEMBER evening, with sky and sea the color of wet cement, and yet the air seemed to crackle with excitement.

"Come in, come in," said Thora, swinging the door of the *Loki* wide open. "If I'd had more warning, I would have vacuumed the Turkish carpet." She raided the cupboards and set out some treats. Then they played games.

Each had their own idea of the sort of things they should do to celebrate everybody's birthday. Lynne wanted to play musical chairs, but there weren't enough chairs. So they played Pin the Tail on the Peacock. But Cosmo didn't like that game. So they tried bobbing for apples. But Thora could stay underwater for such a long time that it wasn't much of a contest. Holly wanted to dress up. Thora handed her an old Halla-Skin. Ricky donned one of Mr. Walters's old peaked caps. Lynne found a matador's vest that Halla had been awarded in Pamplona. Thora took a photograph of her friends with Mr. Walters's Instamatic camera and, after they'd watched the image of themselves develop, Thora slipped it into her now thick journal.

"What's that?" asked Lynne.

"An account of my life and times," replied Thora.

"Can I have a look?"

"Another day," said Thora, tucking her book away under her pillow. Then she announced that she would make the birthday cake. While she busied herself in the kitchen, the children feasted on cucumber sandwiches and miniature gherkins. When they became thirsty, Thora poured them long glasses of tonic water. "Nothing like it to quench a desert thirst." She stirred in scoops of vanilla ice cream to remove the bitterness and brightened the whole thing up with slices of canned beetroot.

While the cake baked, Thora suggested they take a little boat ride. "Yippee!" shouted Ricky.

"I'll sail. Life jackets, everybody!"

Soon they were gliding through the harbor into the open sea. Thora was a confident sailor. It was a cold, moonless, breathless, starless night.

The sea stretched on forever like dark, wrinkled velvet. Thora dropped anchor.

"I'm scared," said Holly.

"There's no one by that name in here!" sang Thora,

returning to the cabin kitchen and producing from the oven a slightly sunken angel food cake. "No matter, we'll build it up again with whipped cream and candles, and nobody will know the difference."

They sang "Happy Birthday" and blew out the candles and tucked into their cake.

"Ouch!" cried Holly, leaping up. "I've bitten something hard!"

"Don't swallow it, whatever you do!" said Thora.

Holly held up a small white pearl. She nibbled it. "Is it real?"

"What other kind of pearl is there?"

"I might have choked!" said Holly. "Why did you put it in?"

"I put in dozens of them. I wanted to make a polka-dot cake, but there weren't any polka dots left and we were clear out of confetti."

"I've got one too!" cried Lynne.

"You'll each have a handful before the cake is finished," said Thora. "Keep them. They make good substitutes for marbles."

She got up and put one of Mr. Walters's records on the record player. "Strangers in the Night" swirled through the cabin.

"And now for the main attraction." She peeled away the

Turkish carpet to reveal, on the floor, the great, round, dark window to the sea.

"What on earth is it?" asked Holly.

"What in *sea*, you mean." Thora pulled open the Plexiglas cover and pressed a red button. "Come and look for yourself!"

A great cone of light stretched from the floor of the *Loki* all the way down to the dark floor of the sea.

There was a dazzled hush.

There were small fish that looked like pink beetles and large fish that resembled electric handsaws. There were blowfish and eels and sea cows. And there were a thousand flickering shadows on the sea floor.

Two octopuses swam into the column of light holding sticks. They began to joust.

A group of potbellied sea horses swam through the column.

"My mother knew a mer-dwarf who grew up on a sea-horse ranch," said Thora. "She used to ride her sea horse, Simon, to school every day. When Simon had a baby, it was only half a centimeter long! They named it Yves. It ate thirty-six hundred shrimp every day!"

"Simon had a baby?" asked Ricky.

"Yep! The boys have the babies."

"I'm glad I'm not a sea horse," said Ricky.

It was then that a mermaid passed through the cone of light.

With eight eyes peering down at her, it's no wonder she looked startled.

She swam several circles around the cone. Holding her body in the shadow, she stared up at them. Her eyes were large and rather bloodshot, her hair a floating frame of yellow. She waved uncertainly.

"It's a mermaid! It's too bright for her," said Holly. "Can you soften the lights?"

The mermaid looked very upset.

"She's trying to tell you something, Thora!" cried Lynne.

Thora forgot all about being undercover. She got down on her hands and knees and pressed her ear to the hole.

"What is she saying, Thora?" asked Holly.

"Shush!" said Thora.

"Wow," breathed Ricky. "Thora can understand her!"

"Didn't you hear what Thora said?" hissed Lynne. "Be quiet!"

When Thora finally stood up, there was a strange expression on her face.

Holly gazed down into the cone of light. The mermaid had fled. "Where did she go? What's wrong, Thora? What did she say to you?"

Thora scratched hard at her elbows.

Holly stamped her foot. "Aren't you going to tell us what is going on?"

"Why do you want to know?" said Thora, wringing her hands.

"What is it?" said Lynne softly.

Thora was too upset to hold back. "My mother lives on the Rock," she said, eyes darting uncertainly from Lynne to Ricky to Holly. "But she hasn't been seen all day. That mermaid is her friend. She's afraid something has happened . . . something bad. I must find her."

Nobody said a word. The cold, moonless, starless night pressed down on them. Excitement had turned to fear.

CHAPTER
43

EVERYBODY WAS PLANNING TO ATTEND THE opening of the Mermaid Cinema.

The mayor, Grimus Grubb, and his wife, Honey. The chief of police. The harbormaster and his assistant. The school principal, Mr. Mason. The baker at Gulli's Goodies. The fishmonger. The taxicab driver. The fishermen who worked on the boats. Even Mrs. Valihora, the landlady from the now-demolished Blue Bell Bed and Breakfast.

Anybody who was anybody, and everybody else as well. The special guests received personal invitations in the mail; the rest found flyers stuffed into their letter boxes.

Some were going because they wanted to be seen. Some in order to see. Many were going in order to eat as many onion rings and popcorn balls as they could. Free of charge.

FROOTY DE MARE
INVITES YOU TO ATTEND
THE GRAND OPENING OF
THE MERMAID CINEMA.
Come and CELEBRATE.
You won't regret it.
FREE ONION RINGS AND ALL-YOU-CAN-EAT
POPCORN BALLS.
PLUS a show that will AMAZE
AND A BIG SURPRISE THAT WILL DELIGHT.
MONEY-BACK GUARANTEE

And *everybody* was curious to see Frooty's "Big Surprise."

It had been a very long time since something fun had occurred in this sleepy seaside town. The air was electric. Frooty was not exactly popular in Grimli. But you had to hand it to him. He knew how to throw a party.

Mrs. Grubb brought out her furs.

The chief of police polished his boots.

Mrs. Rukle booked another appointment at the hairdresser.

And Mr. Rukle laid out a clean shirt. He even thought about scraping the dirt from under his fingernails with an old carving knife. He hadn't eaten a proper meal since Mrs. Rukle left with the children, and the thought of all that free food made the veins in his temples throb.

Only the Greenberg sisters, back now from Venice, had been excluded.

A large neon sign had been placed near the entrance to the new cinema. In bold orange neon lights it read *Banished*.

And beneath it appeared the names FLOSSIE, DOTTIE, and LOTTIE GREENBERG.

The sisters didn't want to go anyway. They dashed off a quick note explaining why.

Mr. de Mare,

There is no way we would lower ourselves to set foot in the Mermaid Cinema. No self-respecting film lover could stand your grotesque taste in films. You can't fool us. We know your movies have been pirated illegally from late-night television and that your curtains and chair coverings are made out of polyester (a high fire danger!) and that your marine murals have been painted directly onto Styrofoam walls (another fire hazard). You couldn't pay us to watch one of your vulgar movies or eat one of your disgusting popcorn balls.

Nothing you could do would amaze us.

Lottie, Dottie and Flossie Greenberg

P.S. We will <u>never ever ever</u> close the Allbent Cinema, so dream on.

CHAPTER

44

IT WAS THE MORNING OF FROOTY'S cinema opening. Thora jumped out of bed and ran as fast as she could to the beach.

It was a mild, overcast day and the water should have felt warm. Instead, it was so icy that it took her breath away. Within seconds her body felt numb and her teeth began to chatter.

Although the Rock was hidden in mist, she knew its exact latitude and longitude without really having to think. A smoke-colored fog was rolling in, and she felt the rip tugging at her as she swam. The swimming was hard going. She felt the water trying to rob her of strength and purpose.

She had considered taking the *Loki* to the Rock the night before to check on her mother, but with all of her friends aboard she had decided against it. Their parents would be wondering where they were. And what if Holly couldn't handle it? Thora wasn't sure how Holly would react.

It had been midnight before she'd returned to the Grimli pier and waved good-bye to her tired and confused friends. It had been far too late and too dark even for a half-mermaid to attempt the swim out to the Rock. She hadn't taken the boat out again because she couldn't risk having it spotted by anybody. But it had been a terrible, sleepless night—the worst of her life.

She approached the Rock now from the north side, where the ramp was, and searched the edge for a toehold. Then she hoisted herself onto the sloping ramp and scrambled up, calling, "Mother, where are you?"

The mist was clearing, and now she could see quite plainly that she was alone.

Calming herself, Thora called to her mother once more. Again, no reply.

A knife edge of fear ran down her chest and legs and into her toes. She trembled—more from fear than cold. Something bad had happened, she knew.

She searched every inch of the Rock, careful not to tread on any of the pointy bits or slippery patches. She stepped sideways along the little rock ledge on the south side. Her eyes ran along the serrated edges, taking in the sea anemones, the dead crabs, the water beetles and rock spiders, the peaty pebbles and stunted grass and tussocks. The toothlike stones around the edge had taken on the appearance of fangs.

Each second felt like an eternity.

Just when she was giving up hope, her eye fell on a scattering of iridescent blue-purple scales. She got down on her knees and examined them closely. They were Halla's, all right. There were handfuls of them. She followed the trail. It led her to the sharply plunging edge on the other side and, peering over it, she saw that there were still more floating in the water below.

Sometimes Halla shed scales when she was grooming herself. Maybe it was nothing.

But then her eye fell on a clump of yellow between two wet rocks. With her heart pounding, she gathered it up, hoping that it might be just a clot of seaweed.

She inhaled.

It smelled of pumpkin pie.

At that moment, Frooty's plane passed overhead, a white banner streaming in its wake. Thora hid in a crack, hoping not to be seen. The plane did a series of somersaults. The white banner tumbled behind it and then flattened out enough for Thora to read its message:

TONIGHT'S THE NIGHT. YOU WON'T BELIEVE YOUR EYES!

CHAPTER

45

THEY WERE ALL WAITING FOR THORA on the deck of the *Loki* when she returned from the Rock—Holly, Ricky, Lynne, and Cosmo. When she saw them, she slipped on her wind-surfing slippers. They made a sad *smuch! smuch!* sound as she walked toward her friends.

"Thora!" Holly threw both arms around her. "Oh, I've been so worried! I've had the most terrible feeling that something bad has happened. Lynne and Ricky came by this morning when they couldn't find you on the *Loki*. Cosmo just shook his head when we asked where you were."

"We thought you might have canoed out to the Rock," said Ricky.

"You've been swimming," said Lynne. "Was she there?"

Thora's bottom lip quivered. She plunged her face into her hands.

"Whatever is wrong?" cried Holly. "Oh, someone please, pretty please, tell me what is going on!" She sat beside Thora. "Lynne and Ricky know something that I don't. They said you must tell me yourself. Please, Thora, tell me and let us help you!"

Ricky now approached Thora. "Take off your slippers," he said.

"Not on your life," said Thora.

Ricky then leaned over and kissed her on the cheek.

Mr. Walters had often kissed Thora on the cheek. But Ricky's kiss was something entirely different. Despite her terrible, wet, unhappy state, she felt the heat creep up her face in a very human blush.

"I think it will help her understand if she knows what you are," he said.

Thora hesitated. She scratched both her elbows. Finally she removed her shoes.

Holly stared at Thora's purple feet. Her long toes. Her scales.

"I'm half-mermaid," explained Thora.

Everyone held their breath, waiting for Holly to either shriek in horror or begin to cry.

She did neither. Rather, she tucked her hair behind her ears and faced Thora squarely. She nodded matter-of-factly. Her calm surprised Thora and encouraged her to continue. "Remember what your father said yesterday about a 'big surprise'?"

Holly's eyes clouded.

"He was all covered with seaweed, remember?"

"Yes, yes," she said. Her face had grown very pale. "The marvelous, magical thing . . ." she managed.

Thora nodded.

Outside, Cosmo was perched on the roof, his tail feathers hanging down the side of the cabin. He leaned over, his long blue neck stretching in Thora's direction and his eyes full of sympathy.

"My mother."

Holly stared hard at her feet. Ricky and Lynne put a hand on each of her shoulders.

"Don't look so miserable," Thora said, trying to give them the thumbs-up. But this time, her thumbs didn't work at all.

Thora did not like to see her friends looking so sad. But she knew that they would not be able to help her with a problem like this. The only people who might be able to help, she hadn't even met yet.

CHAPTER
46

AT THE ALLBENT CINEMA THE LIGHTS were on, but nobody answered her knock. She'd heard that the sisters had come back from Venice, but each time she'd dropped by Kat had told her to go away. Once she'd even chased her off with a broom.

Thora peered in. The blackboard was still there. Under the word *Banished* were two names: Frooty de Mare's and her own.

She waited, Cosmo standing loyally at her side, for what seemed a very long time. She was not sure how well her father had known the sisters, only that he had worked at the cinema. She wondered if they would even remember him.

Eventually three figures, returning from their morning walk, crunched toward her across the gravel. Their noses and cheeks were rosy. They slowed down and stopped talking when they saw Thora.

With her wet ponytail falling into her face and her well-worn Halla-Skin still dripping from her swim out to the Rock, Thora *was* a strange sight. She imagined what she must look like to their eyes and wished she'd taken the time to change and spruce herself up a bit. So much for good impressionistics!

"The matinee doesn't start until one o'clock," said the tallest and the most serious-looking of the sisters. She had a long nose and wore stylish red-framed glasses like the ones that Thora had seen on the reporters in Milan, after Halla had swum the Rubicon. From what Mr. Walters had told her of the sisters, Thora guessed that this one was Lottie.

"She's soaking wet—she's shivering," said the smallest sister, who must be Dottie.

"Her lips are blue," said the third, obviously Flossie.

There was no time to waste on chitchat. "I've come to talk to you about Thor," said Thora.

Astonished, they all said the name together. "Thor?"

"He used to work here. Do you remember him?"

"Why?" asked Dottie cagily. "What do you know of him?"

"Quite a lot, on the one hand. Nothing, on the other. I've never met him. He disappeared before I was even born."

"Is this some sort of hoax?" snapped Lottie, her face stern as a rock sculpture.

"Not that I know of."

"Who sent you?"

Thora considered their question carefully. "Nobody. I'm his *daughter*. My name is Thora."

The sisters looked in the direction of the blackboard, where Kat had written Thora's name.

"My mother told me he once worked here. She told me I should come to you if I got into trouble."

"Who *is* your mother?" demanded Lottie.

"Halla."

"Let's go where we can talk," said Lottie, unlocking the door of the cinema.

Thora followed Lottie and the two other sisters, Dottie and Flossie, down a dark corridor to a fragrant and spacious kitchen with an enormous stove. Thora felt better immediately. The room was furnished with a table and painted blue chairs and countertops cluttered with gleaming saucepans and other cooking utensils. There was also an antique-looking high chair that seemed as if it hadn't been used in many, many years. The photos of movie stars that hung on the wall were faint with age. Thora could only just make out the writing:

To Dottie, KEEP SMILING. Clark Gable
Love you Dottie, don't ever change.
Frank S.

✩ ✩ ✩

Dottie passed Thora a soft, fleecy blanket. Once the tea was served, Lottie sat down in front of Thora. She sat very straight and took a deep breath. "So," she said. "Thor's daughter."

Thora nodded.

"What sort of age are you?"

"Ten years and one month."

"Your mother is really Halla?"

Tears welled in Thora's eyes as she thought of her mother. "Yes."

Lottie pursed her lips and then continued with her questions. "How can you prove this?"

Thora pulled off one of her slippers and waggled her toes. The cold had turned her feet and ankles an especially violent shade of purple.

The sisters leaned forward.

Lottie nodded. "Mermaid." It was a statement of fact.

Nobody said anything for a moment.

"Well, technically speaking, I am *half*-mermaid," Thora said. "As you can see, I don't have a tail."

Flossie giggled nervously. Dottie began to sob.

"Hush," said Lottie. "Do you have any *more* proof?"

Thora pointed to the floor. "See that puddle?"

"That's why Kat banished her," said Dottie thoughtfully.

Thora shrugged and said, "Well, my mother *did* tell me humans could be funny about this sort of thing. . . ."

She unfastened her ponytail. She had spent so much effort *hiding* her mermaidness that it felt strange to be showing it off! And yet it was also a tremendous relief.

It took a few seconds to get her blowhole revved up. The water trickled out in a thin stream.

"My goodness," said Lottie.

Then *whoosh!* A great torrent of water gushed out as if from a strong garden hose.

Lottie was too startled to duck out of the way. Her glasses flew off her nose. She blinked the water out of her eyes. Her hair lay flat on top of her head.

"So it's true!" said Flossie excitedly.

"Oh, I *am* sorry," said Thora. "I'm a little rusty. It's been ages since I've used my jet stream. . . ."

Lottie shook her head. "Don't worry. I'll dry."

Dottie now took charge. Her red-rimmed eyes burned into Thora. "We thought you were a spy for Frooty de Mare. That he'd named you Thora—to echo the name of our own Thor—as part of a cruel joke."

"While we were away, the girl who works for us, Kat, reported that a girl calling herself Thora kept showing up here," added Flossie. "She said she'd banished you for spilling your drink, but you kept returning. That sort of per-sistence has a Frooty de Mare quality about it, and it set off the alarm bells. We just didn't think that you might be . . ."

The two other sisters suddenly lost all their reserve. Tears now sprang into their eyes as well. Then Dottie reached out and embraced Thora. She stroked her head. She almost squeezed her half to death! "My granddaughter."

CHAPTER
47

WHEN THORA WAS SMALL, SHE HAD often dreamed of a moment when she would find herself surrounded by family, everybody hugging, crying, and telling each other how much they loved one another.

What she hadn't anticipated was how strange it was to learn that she had a surname!

Thora *Greenberg*!

As Dottie embraced her, Thora chuckled to herself. No, it was not how she had dreamed it. It was much, much, much better! She pinched herself on the arm. "Ouch!" she cried.

"Why did you do that?" asked Flossie, horrified.

"I want to make sure that this is not just a wonderful dream that I am going to wake up from."

When long-lost relatives are brought together, they often just like to sit and stare at one another, to bask in each other's gaze the way a fish might linger in a sunny spot.

Dottie, Lottie, Flossie, and Thora did just that. They had so much to tell one another and so much to ask that they didn't know where to start. Questions and answers kept dissolving into tears, hugs, and laughter. Then Flossie got it into her head that Thora must eat, and so she busied herself making one of her soups. Dottie sat as close as possible to Thora, as if she meant to inhale her. Lottie chattered away about how they had given up hope of ever seeing Thor again, and *now his very own daughter was seated right before them, with eyes the very same color as Thor's as well as his funny habit of scratching his elbows!*

"He loved Flossie's soups," said Dottie.

"Especially my turnip soup. Try it. You look like you need some." Flossie handed Thora a bowl.

"We hoped to give him the cinema to run as his own."

"He was the best projectionist in the business," said Dottie.

"It's all computerized now. We haven't kept up."

"But your father would have!"

"He was so clever!"

"One day he came to work and announced that he had met the woman he wanted to marry."

"He had caught her in his fishing net."

"He was smitten."

"'Head over tails' is how my mother put it," said Thora between gulps.

"We were very pleased for him. Admittedly, we worried a little when we learned that Halla was a mermaid."

"Yes," said Flossie. "Humans and mermaids are like oil and water."

"We didn't say that to him, of course."

"Young people have to find things out for themselves."

"And he was so happy."

"He warned us that he had to be very careful. We would have liked a big wedding, but he explained that they would have to get married in secret."

"We agreed to meet him at the *Loki* the night after the wedding. We wanted to meet his bride and give her a gift. But they never showed up."

"We went back the next day."

"And the next."

"A few months later, the harbormaster suggested we put the *Loki* up for sale."

"I couldn't. It felt too much like giving up on him."

"We know nothing about boats," said Lottie. "The Allbent was losing money."

"We made the harbormaster promise not to sell it to Frooty de Mare," added Flossie.

Thora squeezed Dottie's hand. "You don't know what happened to him, do you?"

"We'll find out one day," replied Dottie tenderly. "I know it."

"Then one night, less than a year on, a tall man dressed in white knocked on the window."

"A perfect English gent," said Flossie.

"Mr. Walters!" cried Thora.

"At first we thought it very peculiar."

"Looking for milk in the middle of the night."

"But when we learned it was for a hungry baby girl, we let him in."

"We gave him some baby things. A blanket, a rattle, a milk bottle . . ."

"And a bunny rabbit!" cried Thora excitedly. There was a ripping sound as Thora pulled open one of the Velcro pockets on her Halla-Skin and fished out a piece of old fur for the sisters to inspect. It was neither blue nor yellow, but something in between. "The rabbit!" she said. "It's been everywhere with me, even Timbuktu!"

Dottie sighed. "It was your father's."

Lottie continued with the story. "Mr. Walters came by the next day to thank us. He was just so . . ."

"Dreamy!" exclaimed Flossie.

"That same day, the *Loki* sailed away. We learned he had bought it."

"He sent Flossie postcards from around the world."

"From Finland one year, Japan another."

"One year from Tahiti!"

"He said he was keeping an eye on his fairy godchild and her mother."

"He never mentioned you or your mother by name. We had no idea."

"His last postcard was from Argentina," said Flossie.

"His brother died," said Thora. "He'll be back soon."

"And what about your mother?" Lottie asked innocently.

Tears welled in Thora's eyes. The time had come to tell them her great problem. "I don't know where she is!"

"You don't *know*?"

"Not for certain. You see, she was living on the Rock, but she's not there anymore. I just swam out this morning

205

and couldn't find her. But I'm almost positive that she's been captured—that Frooty de Mare's going to do something with her at the opening of the Mermaid Cinema!"

"Frooty!" yelped Flossie. "That bauble-nosed bandit!"

The sisters asked Thora detailed questions about her encounters with Frooty. They wanted to know everything. Then Dottie glanced at her watch. "The cinema opening is in an hour's time!"

Lottie pursed her lips again. "Well, it certainly sounds like Frooty is behind all of this. No doubt it's another one of his cruel pranks. He's been casting about for years to find a way to close us down. Of course he waited until we were away to launch his ridiculous new theater. I reckon he's gone too far this time. What do you think, girls?"

Flossie and Dottie nodded in agreement.

"What should I do?" asked Thora anxiously.

"You must go to the opening of the Mermaid Cinema. We've been banned from attending."

"Not that we would ever dream of setting foot in one of his vile establishments anyway," said Flossie hotly.

"True," said Lottie. "Now when you see your mother, you must pass this on to her," said Lottie. She indicated for everybody to follow her out of the kitchen and up a set of rickety stairs to the projectionist's room. The walls were lined with reels and camera equipment. Lottie leaned over and unscrewed a ring from the main projector. She gave it a quick polish on the sleeve of her sweater and passed it to Thora.

"It was supposed to be your parents' wedding gift," said Flossie. "But we never had a chance to give it to them."

Thora held it up. "It's warm," she said.

"So it should be," said Lottie. "It's the projectionist's ring. It has been used to filter all the magic of cinema in this theater since the day we opened. So many hopes, dreams, promises, disappointments, tears, and mysteries have passed through that ring that it's surprising it's still able to keep its shape."

Thora turned it around and peered through it at the sisters. "What will it do?"

"It's magic," said Flossie.

"Not so much magic," said Dottie. "More like good luck."

"It really depends," said Lottie.

"Your father was steeped in the magic of this cinema," said Dottie. "He's the expert on the subject."

"Then why didn't it help to find my father?"

Flossie sneezed. "Well, it's not necessarily a missing person sort of magic."

"It tends to flicker a little," said Dottie.

"Put it on," urged Lottie. "If it hums, it's on your side."

It was far too large for Thora's ring finger, so she slipped it onto her wrist. Instantly she felt a faint vibrating sensation.

"It might help you sort out this business with Frooty. I like to believe that it's helped us deal with him for years." The twinkle in Lottie's eyes put Thora at ease.

"Go on," said Dottie, biting her lip to try to stop the tears from welling up in her eyes. "If only we could go with you!"

FROOTY WAS RUSHING ABOUT THE GREAT foyer of the new Mermaid Cinema when the phone call came.

An English voice said, "Mr. de Mare?"

"Speaking," said Frooty.

"It's Wally Jack. I'll be there in one hour. Just left the airport."

"Ten-four," said Frooty. He grabbed hold of Mrs. de Mare and gave her a hug. "We scored, tweety bird!" he exclaimed. "The great BBC news reporter, Mr. Wally Jack, has traveled all the way from *London* to cover our story!"

"Well, I should hope so," sniffed Mrs. de Mare. "After all, this is *international news.*"

CHAPTER
49

FROOTY WAS ON TOP OF THE WORLD.

All the people who had doubted him and criticized him and even *laughed* at him were now *pouring* into his cinema. There was nothing like a good party to make people forget they didn't like you! Look at them stuffing themselves on the free onion rings, popcorn balls, and blue licorice bluebottles.

Soon everybody would be milling about in the Sea King Games Room (another unique feature of the Mermaid Cinema!), throwing away their money on the slot machines. *Spending, spending, spending!* Just think how they would spend once they saw the main attraction!

There would be busloads of tourists from all over the country.

Chartered jets full of wealthy foreigners with fat wallets.

Frooty grew a little dizzy thinking about it.

He snaked expertly through the crowd, passing balloons

to babies, waving modestly to the local television crew. He
would save his biggest smile for the BBC, for Mr. Wally Jack.

This was his dream come true.

One day in the not-so-distant future, people would
figure out that he was a genius.

His thoughts galloped ahead. He imagined tomorrow's
headlines: FROOTY DE MARE,

CINEMA KING OF THE 21ST
CENTURY.

First, Grimli.

Then the world!

All these twit-brained lumpfish were in for a *big surprise*.

CHAPTER
50

OUTSIDE THE ALLBENT, THORA AND COSMO sat on a bench, still absorbing the conversation with the sisters. On Thora's wrist, the projectionist's ring felt warm. It resembled the Indian bracelet given to her mother by a friend from Simla: a thick copper band about one inch thick with an oddly delicate serrated edge. She removed it and peered inside. It had been engraved:

To the marriage of Earth and Sea

It was sad to think that the gift had never been given to her parents. Perhaps it explained why the Allbent tended to show rather sad films these days. "Thor was of the earth and Halla of the sea," she said to Cosmo. "That makes me a bit of both." And holding that thought as carefully as she held the projectionist's ring, she made her way back to the beach and walked along the pebbly shore.

Half of the land. Half of the sea. Half dry, half wet.

Human and mermaid. Thora. Me.

It was Cosmo who broke her reverie. She was startled by the distance she had traveled along the shore. She refastened her ponytail and, with a surge of purpose, she and Cosmo jogged back to join the crowd that had gathered around the Mermaid Cinema.

A three-piece Dixieland band had been set up on the front patio of the new building. Thora was disturbed to see that the musicians were dressed up as mermaids, their legs stuffed into long green tails, their hair (most certainly wigs!) tumbling over their shoulders. A lurid neon sign blinked THE MERMAID CINEMA. The license plate on a long, white stretch limousine in front read CINEMA KING.

"It reminds me of the Motel Skwander in Las Vegas," Thora said to Cosmo. "The tinfoily effect."

Cosmo spread his tail and nodded.

They walked past a camera crew and up the stairs into a foyer, the Popcorn Hall. Large banquet tables heaved with food. The air was prickly with onion gas and the slightly eggy stench of not-so-freshly-popped popcorn. Everybody was talking and chewing and swallowing at once.

"Oh, look!" Thora said to Cosmo. "It's Mrs. Grubb."

In addition to her silly germ-repelling face mask, Mrs. Grubb was wearing green eye shadow and a fluffy pink cardigan.

"Ah," said Mrs. Grubb. "Surprise, surprise. It's our sickly little orphan girl. Do you realize that what you did to the Rukles when you ran off like that was not only rude and ungrateful, but had tragic consequences for the Rukle family?"

"You mean Mr. Rukle had no money that night for the slot machines?"

Mr. Rukle then appeared at Mrs. Grubb's side. "She made my wife and children leave me. Now I have nothing."

He buried his face in his hands and began to cry.

"See?" said Mrs. Grubb. "Reducing a grown man to tears! What will your next prank be? I am very disappointed in you, Thora. Nobody tried harder than me to help you."

Mr. Rukle stuffed something into his trouser pocket. "Whaddina dog's breakfast are *you* staring at?" he demanded. The veins in his temples throbbed accusingly.

"I believe you have an allergy to onion rings," replied Thora. "Maybe you ought to borrow a pair of my goggles! Mr. Walters wears them when he chops onions!"

Mrs. Grubb made a *humph* noise. "I want you to know, little missy, that I am not finished with you yet. Not surprisingly, it's been impossible to find another family who will take you on. But I do not give up easily."

"Thora has a family already," a voice suddenly quipped. It was Holly.

"I would advise you to mind your own business, Miss de Mare," snapped Mrs. Grubb. "And does your father have any idea who you are consorting with?"

"Frankly, Mrs. Grubb," said Holly with a dimpled smile, "I don't give a damn."

Thora couldn't believe her ears.

Mrs. Grubb sputtered. "Rude girl!"

"Thora is my best friend on earth," continued Holly, loud enough to turn heads. "Next to Lynne and Ricky Rukle, of course. Come on, Thora. Let's get something to eat."

Holly's words took Thora by surprise. *My best friend on earth!* Nobody her age had ever said such a nice thing about her. The ring on her wrist hummed. How was it that terrible things could happen at the same time as wonderful things? Bad and good together. Life was very strange.

At that moment, the Rukle children came bounding toward them.

"Thora!" they cried. "Are we glad to see you! What did the Greenberg sisters say?"

The children huddled in the corner of the foyer. Thora spoke fast, in a whisper. There was not enough time to tell them everything, but she showed them the projectionist's ring and let them feel the magical warmth it emanated.

Ricky leaned forward and impulsively planted a kiss on Thora's cold cheek. Thora felt that same mysterious heat rising on her face.

The crackle of a microphone put an end to the pleasant interlude. They each grabbed a bucket of popcorn balls and went to join the crowd.

CHAPTER
51

FROM A PLATFORM AT THE BACK of the cinema foyer, Frooty fiddled with the microphone. "Ladies and gentlemen, boys and girls, while we wait for Mr. Wally Jack, the great foreign news reporter from London, I would like to welcome you all to the great Mermaid Cinema."

He pointed to a large screen on the wall behind him. "Let me draw your attention to all the wonderful new features of this great modern cinema. Unlike the Allbent, this building was built especially to show you the latest films from Hollywood. It features three viewing theaters with snazzy red velvet seats."

"We peeked inside," whispered Lynne. "The theaters are so small they'll give everyone claustrophobia. They'll have to squish in like sardines!"

"And the seats are *fake* velvet," said Ricky.

Frooty continued. "In keeping with my interest in aquatic motifs, neon lighting experts have created these visually stunning displays of marine life for you to enjoy while you line up to see your film. In no other cinema in the world can you see such original use of neon! Oh, and the snack bar will offer you an astonishing range of treats: popcorn, of course, but also fish-shaped drops, buttermallow squid, chocolate starfish, and our very own jellied mermaids—invented by our resident sweets expert, Mr. Siegfried Twizzle!

There was a burst of applause for a roly-poly man in a white tuxedo.

"Now Mr. Wally Jack will be here any minute. But let us delay no further. This is the moment you have all been waiting for. *The Big Surprise*. Let us all stand back a little to make room. Any pushing or shoving and you will be asked to leave."

Thora and her friends exchanged glances.

Suddenly there came a great creaking, squeaking, splashing sound. Six people, including Madge, wearing a sparkly green top adorned with a cardboard dorsal fin, were rolling into the main foyer what appeared to be an enormous rectangular box on wheels. It was the size of a moving truck and covered with red-and-white-striped wrapping paper. A large pink bow sat on the top.

Everyone whispered at once.

Up on the podium, Frooty de Mare looked very happy. Mrs. de Mare also looked very happy. They seemed to grow taller, wider, and happier as they looked out at the crowd.

"Ladies and gentlemen," said Frooty, "I am not a poet, darn it. I wish I were. Like you, I am a simple man. A man with a dream."

He dabbed his eye with a handkerchief.

Thora wondered if he too was using an onion to make his tears.

"May I invite my daughter and her little friends to step forward and remove the wrapping paper?" He flashed them a piratical grin.

Holly, Thora, Lynne, and Ricky joined hands and stepped forward.

Thora was the tallest. She reached up and took hold of the bow. She pulled. There was a ripping sound. She looked around.

"Now wait a minute," said Frooty.

The crowd urged her on. The room pulsed with

curiosity. Everyone was desperate to know. *What was it?*

Thora continued pulling and ripping. In the strip where the paper had been removed, glass.

"An aquarium?" guessed Ricky.

Now all the children grabbed handfuls of paper. They tore and they ripped. Soon the floor was a sea of red and white paper.

A thick silence fell.

"Wow!" said Ricky.

Dimly, Thora registered the roar of astonishment and excitement. People were clapping. Talking. Corks popped, and outside firecrackers sizzled in the sky.

WHIZZZZ. BOOOM. WHIZZZZA. KABOOOM.

Thora felt as if she were swimming through cotton wool.

She stepped up close and pressed her face against the cold glass.

"Mother," she whispered. "It really is you."

CHAPTER

52

HALLA LOOKED TERRIBLE.

Topped with a plastic tiara, her beautiful blonde hair had been sprayed with glitter and her tail had lost its shimmer.

It was as if she'd been beached and bleached—which, as she would later tell Thora and Mr. Walters, is pretty much what happened when she was captured by Frooty and the coast guard and hauled over to the Mermaid Cinema to be displayed in a tank of polluted water.

"How awful, how terrible," said Holly. "Even worse than I imagined."

"Oh, Thora!" cried Lynne. "Your poor mother!"

"We've got to get her out," said Ricky.

Frooty's voice boomed over the loudspeaker. "Okay, tweety birds, let's move back from the aquarium. Let everyone get a view. Only fair!"

Thora tried to climb into the tank. "Help me!"

"Get down!" ordered Frooty. "Step aside. Let the journalists in with their cameras. Do you hear me?"

Holly, Ricky, and Lynne tried to lift Thora. She reached up to the top of the tank but couldn't get a grip. Some sort of plastic screen was acting as a lid, and there was nowhere to get a foothold on the slippery glass. She slid back down.

A photographer from the *Daily Seasider* began to shout. "Get those brats out of the way. I don't have all day!"

People swarmed around.

Halla tried to leap up the side of the tank, but she was too weak. She swam in confused circles in the murky water.

Thora could see that her mother was very ill. She'd seen her like this twice before: once while on tour in Alaska in the freezing cold, and another time after swimming in the filthy Danube River near the Hungarian border, when her tail became fouled with oil. Perhaps the water in the tank was not even salt water!

Mother and daughter stared helplessly at each other. Halla had never looked so sad. Were those tears? Was the water level rising?

But mermaids didn't cry.

It was a fact.

So what was this?

"Any minute now, folks . . . the great BBC newsman will be here!"

"A world exclusive!" shouted Mrs. de Mare.

"Stand back, everybody!"

"He's here. Hurrah!"

"Mr. Wally Jack!"

Thora felt Frooty's hands on her shoulders.

"Move on. Let the reporter through."

Thora tried to wriggle away when she noticed that the ring on her wrist was vibrating, growing lighter in color and warmer by the second. Now it seemed to be boiling with anger. It was how *she* felt too!

She slipped the ring off her wrist and passed it to Holly. "Put it on Cosmo's beak!" she whispered.

Without the ring on her wrist, Frooty was stronger than

anything she'd ever encountered. He was hauling her away. Through the crowd, she saw Holly stepping up to Cosmo to fit the ring on his beak as Thora had requested.

"Use your beak, Cosmo!" Thora hollered. "Use your beak!"

Frooty dumped Thora into the cinema kitchen and slammed the door.

"Ow!" she cried, landing heavily against a huge industrial popcorn machine. "I've burned myself!"

She examined her arm, but it was not a burn at all.

On her wrist was a mark left by the projectionist's ring.

With renewed strength, she jumped up and pushed against the blocked door. To her surprise, it opened.

She was just in time to see a tall man dressed in white weaving his way through the crowd. Not as agile as he'd once been, but with a stride determined and confident.

He wore a lettuce-green fedora on his head. A camera was slung at a jaunty angle over his shoulder.

"Mr. Wally Jack!" said Frooty, immensely relieved.

But Thora knew it was Mr. Walters.

The crowd parted to let him through.

Frooty rushed back to the podium. "Welcome, Mr. Jack!" he said, and handed him the microphone.

The man nodded. He regarded the crowd with his rather

popping blue eyes. "This place that Frooty de Mare has called the Mermaid Cinema is a truly vile establishment," he announced.

His voice had all the authority of a veteran newsman.

A surprised hush fell over the room. Frooty's mouth hung open.

"Cosmo?" Mr. Walters said. "Didn't you hear what Thora said? Use your beak, bird!" Mr. Walters commanded.

Cosmo stood tall before the aquarium—almost a meter in height.

He puffed out his chest, spread his tail, drew back his aristocratic head, and then, with one hard forward rap, dashed his beak against the glass.

CHAPTER
53

EVEN THE GREENBERG SISTERS HEARD THE *CRACK*.

The unmistakable sound of an aquarium splitting down the middle. With slightly trembling hands, Lottie passed Flossie her opera glasses and urged her to take a look.

They were really too old to be sitting on the roof.

What if one of them fell off?

But when the call had come in from Mr. Walters that afternoon, shortly after Thora's visit, they'd donned their warm pink tracksuits and packed a picnic basket with a thermos of hot chocolate, three tin cups, granola bars, stopwatch, blankets, hats, and a Polaroid camera. Then they'd closed the cinema until further notice and climbed up onto its sloping, tiled roof to watch and wait.

Over the telephone Mr. Walters couldn't say for sure how it would all turn out, but he had promised them a show they would never forget.

They hadn't been disappointed.

"Life really is much more more *thrilling* than fiction," Dottie would reflect later. Even though Lottie considered such statements to be worn-out clichés (especially considering that her sister had got the phrase wrong), she had to admit that what they'd witnessed was as good as any of the movies that had flickered across their dusty old screen for some thirty years.

At approximately seven in the evening, Mr. Walters had cantered up to the entrance of the Mermaid Cinema on a magnificent horse, followed on foot by an irate policeman in a red tunic with shiny gold buttons. Mr. Walters had proffered the sisters a discreet wave.

His eyes had lingered a little longer on Flossie than the other two—though he hadn't been so corny as to wink or blow a kiss, as Flossie secretly wished he had.

They'd watched him dismount ("so spry for a man his age!" sighed Flossie) and bound up the stairs. In his youth, he'd been a dashing sportsman, coach, and journalist. In middle age, he'd commanded vast audiences with his deep, clean-cut enunciation and crisp diction. And now, in his dramatic return to Grimli, he seemed to display each and every one of the qualities that had been required of him in those demanding professions.

According to Dottie's stopwatch, Mr. Walters had been

inside the Mermaid Cinema for three minutes and twenty-four seconds when the sound of cracking glass reached them.

After four minutes and thirteen seconds, water began to trickle out the front doors of the Mermaid Cinema.

Through a shared lens, the sisters watched the trickle grow to a powerful stream.

The stream to a river.

The river coursed out of the front door and down the steps.

They could not hear people screaming in fright, because it was not really very frightening. The river was well behaved. It formed a sort of elegant pathway leading out of the building. It flowed with the sort of control you associate with rivers that are banked on both sides. It was a friendly sort of river that made you want to jump in for a swim.

Then all three sisters saw them.

Almost directly underneath the cinema, Thora was waving and grinning widely as if she were doing nothing more unusual than riding in a festival float in a town parade. Halla looked up at them and smiled too.

"So *that's* who Thor married."

"Finally we see her!"

"She looks like a very nice mermaid."

"Doesn't she?"

"Now get back from the edge, Dottie."

They watched as the water carried Thora and Halla past the fish shop, the bakery, the hardware store, and down along the Grimli pier. And hurrying it along while at the same time pointing the way was a rather friendly breeze, whose modest goal seemed simply, as Lottie later put it, to deliver its true love and offspring out of harm's way.

Yes, a sensitive breeze, sighed Flossie, that guided the flow of water around the old red oil

drum at the end of the pier ("It could have just
knocked it over, after all!") before finally, gently,
sweetly, and carefully, like a giant's hand,
releasing mother and daughter safely
into the calm of the sea.

CHAPTER
54

The Loki
Somewhere in the Indian Ocean
40 degrees S, 60 degrees E
Speed: 8 knots per hour

Dearest Holly,

How are you, my great and worthy amigo? I hope
this finds you hale and hearty as an Olympic hammer
thrower. We have been sailing hard for three weeks now,
and we think we've outwitted the coast guard. After
Cosmo cracked the aquarium with the help of the
projectionist's ring, we boarded a magic carpet
of water that took us all the way to the
Rock. We did not have to wait long
before we heard, on a mega-
phone, Mr. Walters's heart-
warming "Ahoy!" He lost his

fedora in all the excitement, which is a shame because it was brand-new. And poor Cosmo lost some of his prized eye feathers, which will take a long time to grow back. I don't expect he'll be up to delivering this letter to you. I may have to ask the hungry-looking gull who has been trailing us since we left Grimli.

Our plans are still a little up in the air, so I am not sure when we will see you again. You were such a help, and I miss you very much! I get goose bumps remembering your words. Perhaps that is what having a best friend is meant to feel like. I have told my mother everything about you. She said you sound <u>lovely</u> and she wants you to know that the mermaid who visited us that night on the boat was <u>her</u> best friend, Marina, and you are not to worry about her, because she is safe as a clam on the ocean floor. She thinks you were brave to place the ring on Cosmo's beak. She asks me to pass on her deepest phosphorescence.

Though I am sad that we have been parted, there is a ray of sunshine, too. I am glad that nobody will be trying to make me go to school, or join a frosted family, or any of that other malarkey.

I hope the lunkheads are treating you well. I am enclosing some tips I picked up from Boris the Remarkable, just in case you need to unhypnotize them.

It is very delicious to be reunited with my mother. I do not yet know all the glory details about her capture. She is not the sort of mermaid who likes to dwell in dark pools. But I am returning with this letter three of the six teeth your father lost in his struggle to capture her. My mother has scrubbed them up with a pumice stone and polished them with swordfish oil. You can imagine our surprise when we discovered that they are actually made of gold! Though she does not yet have her shimmer back, she is now in good spirits. She is reading a book about the wind. She just told me that the word cloud is from the Greek word for "buttocks"! She doesn't have buttocks and so she didn't understand why Mr. Walters turned red and had to leave the room when we started to examine the clouds overhead.

So long, my far-flung best friend. Please give my warmest regards to my good mates Ricky and Lynne. I am sure that if Lynne is willing to be shot out of cannons, she will someday make it to the Moscow Circus (though I think I would prefer it if she learned the art of contortion—much less noisy and apt to scare Cosmo). Someday I hope to meet up again with Ricky. Please don't tell a soul, old soul, but he said he'd like to take me to the Rock and kiss me again!

(I still think that swimming with dolphins in Zanzibar would be more fun.)

Farewell!
Write if you remember!
Thora Greenberg
Your best friend
XXXXX

P.S. Please, I beg you never to mention that part about Ricky. It is most definitely highly calcified information!

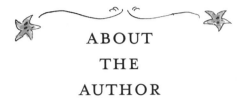

ABOUT
THE
AUTHOR

Gillian Johnson grew up in Winnipeg, Canada. She now lives in England and Tasmania with her husband, writer Nicholas Shakespeare, and their two sons, Max and Benedict. Gillian has written and illustrated numerous books for children, including ROOS IN SHOES by Thomas Keneally.

COMING SOON

THORA AND THE GREEN SEA-UNICORN